# A Farewell to Baker Street

A collection of previously unknown cases from the extraordinary career of Mr Sherlock Holmes

Mark Mower

Paperback ISBN  978-1-78092-844-9
ePub ISBN  978-1-78092-845-6
PDF ISBN  978-1-78092-846-3

Published in the UK by MX Publishing
335 Princess Park Manor, Royal Drive,
London, N11 3GX
www.mxpublishing.co.uk
Cover design by www.staunch.com

# Contents

| | | |
|---|---|---|
| Preface | | 4 |
| 1. | An Affair of the Heart | 7 |
| 2. | The Curious Matter of the Missing Pearmain | 31 |
| 3. | A Study in Verse | 61 |
| 4. | The Case of the Cuneiform Suicide Note | 86 |
| 5. | The Trimingham Escapade | 101 |

# Preface

It is with a very sad heart, yet enormous pride, that I pen these few words in introducing this collection of previously unknown cases from the extraordinary career of Mr Sherlock Holmes. In reality, it would be more appropriate to refer to the '...*extraordinary careers of Mr Sherlock Holmes and his ever-loyal partner, John H Watson, MD.*' as I am firmly of the view that had it not been for the lasting friendship and assiduous note taking, file keeping and penmanship of my late uncle, the consulting detective's fame would have been considerably diminished with the passing of years.

That is not to say that I have anything other than the greatest admiration and respect for Sherlock Holmes. Had it not been for his intervention, the course of my life would have been very different and considerably poorer to be sure. I will say no more of the matter at this stage, for the full details of the case are set out in the narrative which Dr Watson has entitled *An Affair of the Heart* and which forms the first of the tales in this new volume.

My real point is that Watson's role, in many of the conundrums and investigations we have come to know and relish as the enduring performance of a genius, is all too easily overlooked or played down with Holmes taking centre stage. And yet, the good doctor was no mere support act or bit-part player. He was the light to Holmes' darkness and the candle to his flame. The great detective did indeed shine, but it was Watson that provided much of the illumination and kept him firmly in the spotlight.

John Hamish Watson passed away in the early hours of Monday, 6th February 1939, at the age of eighty-six. He is sadly missed by us all. His health had declined rapidly in the two weeks prior to his death, so much so, that when he sent word to me that the bowel cancer he had been diagnosed with some months before had finally placed a firm and irremediable grip on his frail body, I knew that the end was near and raced to be at his bedside. Not once did he complain and not once did he question why it should be at that moment that his own extraordinary life should come to such an end.

My uncle had let it be known a decade earlier that on his death he wished me to be the executor of his will and guardian of all of his personal and pecuniary affairs. One of the tasks he had sanctioned very deliberately was that I should use my discretion in selecting for publication some of the three dozen or so cases where he had assisted Holmes, which had not already seen the light of day for one reason or another. One of these was *The Trimingham Escapade*, which was the last case the pair enjoyed together and one which only reached a point of some conclusion last year. I am delighted to present it in this collection.

The other tales I have chosen for this volume demonstrate more of the critical interplay between the two men which made their partnership so memorable and endearing. *The Curious Matter of the Missing Pearmain* is a murder story to rank alongside the best of the tales being produced by our current crop of 'Golden Age' crime writers, what some authors of American detective fiction might term a locked-room mystery. *The Case of the Cuneiform Suicide Note* is a tale in which Dr Watson uses his expert knowledge to help solve a mystery, while *A Study in Verse* has the pair assisting the Birmingham City Police in a complicated case of robbery which leads them towards a new and dangerous adversary. All are very fine tales.

I am not sure whether the release of any more of these previously unknown cases would be in the public interest. I will determine that in due course, having considered the critical response to this first volume. Either way, I hope I have contributed in some small part to the lasting memory of two extraordinary men.

Christopher Henry Watson, MD

Bexley Heath, Kent – 15th February 1939

# 1. An Affair of the Heart

In my long association with Sherlock Holmes, I only ever knew him to be an honourable and loyal friend, who could be relied upon to act with the utmost tact and discretion on any matters of a personal nature. So it was that when I found myself embroiled in a distinctly delicate family matter in the autumn of 1886, it was to Holmes that I naturally deferred.

We were sitting in the congenial surroundings of Brown's Hotel in Albemarle Street having just met with the establishment's proprietor in his newly refurbished lounge bar. Holmes had been engaged to tackle a potentially damaging case of jewellery theft from one of the more expensive suites in the hotel, occupied at that time by a crown prince from Eastern Europe. I had high hopes that this would turn out to be a colourful and absorbing episode, which might showcase my friend's remarkable talents. In reality, what I had envisaged somewhat prematurely as *The Curious Case of the Ukrainian Emerald* was solved by Holmes in less than half an hour, leading to the very public arrest by Scotland Yard of both the crown prince and his criminally-complicit manservant. It was clearly not the outcome that the hotel owner had anticipated and, having paid Holmes very discreetly for his services, the red-faced manager left us to finish what remained of our strong Turkish coffee and Panamanian cigars.

Holmes turned towards me with a telling grin. "Not one for your journal then, Watson? I fear that a simple case of insurance fraud is unlikely to excite the interests of your expectant readers. Still, while we have a quiet moment, it might be a good time for you to share with me the concerns you have about your nephew Christopher's impending marriage to Mrs Virginia Aston-Cowper."

His offhand comment caught me completely by surprise. "Holmes, I had no idea that you had spoken recently to young Christopher. I do indeed have some reservations about the match, but cannot see how my nephew knows of these – it is a good six months since we last had any sort of conversation. In any case, it was only four days ago that I received the wedding invitation, which, I have to say, came very much out of the blue."

"My dear friend, I have had no such conversation with Christopher. In fact, if you remember, I have only met him but the once, on the infamous occasion that he called upon us at Baker Street, claiming to have lost his wallet and being without the train fare to enable him to get back to his student digs in Oxford."

"Yes, of course," I replied, remembering how embarrassing the incident had been. "Not the first time his excessive gambling has got him into trouble. But how, then, do you know about his recent news and my thoughts on the matter? Please tell me this isn't some elaborate parlour trick on your part."

Holmes laughed heartily. "From a lesser man, I might have taken that as an insult, Watson. There is no trickery I can assure you. As you said, the wedding invitation arrived four days ago. It was the only letter addressed to you from the pile that Mrs Hudson brought up to me that day. I cast a glance at the envelope and then placed it in your post rack."

"I trust you didn't return to the letter and open it without my knowledge?"

"Of course not – the envelope told me all that I needed to know. The letter was postmarked 'Oxford' and the address was written in that small, spidery hand which I have come to recognise as that of your nephew. While you may not see or speak to him often, I have observed that Christopher's letters have been arriving more frequently of late, no doubt linked to his gambling debts, but expressed to you in his polite requests for small amounts of money to support his continuing medical studies at the university. That this particular letter was not one of those regular communiqués was apparent from the oddly-sized envelope, which enclosed a card of some sort. Coupled with the clearly displayed 'RSVP' on the back, it was not hard to discern that this was a wedding invitation. And on reading through the announcements in *The Times* that same day, I couldn't fail to see the notice regarding the forthcoming marriage of 'Mr Christopher Henry Watson of Trinity College, Oxford, to Mrs Virginia Belvedere Aston-Cowper of Bexley Heath, Kent'."

"Very neat, Holmes, but how did you know that I had failed to greet the news with any great relish? It is true, that I have tried to support my nephew through all of the troubles he has encountered since the death of my alcoholic brother. I have a great affection for the boy, especially since he has chosen to devote himself to a course of study which mirrors my own. But this latest caper is indeed troubling. And yet, I cannot recollect saying anything to you about the matter."

"Precisely so, and the very fact which prompted me to take note. It is not every day that one receives an invitation to a family wedding and yet you chose not to mention it. Of late, you have been less garrulous than normal and given to periods of intense introspection. The invitation also required a prompt response - something you would attend to ordinarily by return of post. Thus far, you have seen fit to leave the invitation inside the envelope, which this morning still sat within the letter rack. Lethargy is not a characteristic you are prone to, Watson, so I can only conclude that you have chosen to delay your response, being troubled once again by the imprudence of your nephew."

His pinpoint accuracy in targeting such a raw nerve left me deflated. "I was unaware that my innermost thoughts were so easily exposed," said I. "What do you make of the situation?"

He lent across to the low coffee table in front of us and stubbed out what remained of his cigar. "As you know, I am not given to any moral panics or ethical dilemmas when it comes to affairs of the heart. I do not profess to know what drives a man to declare his undying love for another and be content to live out his existence in the shadow of *a better half*. In this case, I take it that your main concern is the fact that Mrs Aston-Cowper is both a widow and a woman some years older than Christopher?"

"Eighteen years older, to be precise!" My anger had surfaced finally and I could no longer hide my frustrations of late: "Christopher is a rash, happy-go-lucky, sort of fellow. But his heart has always been in the right place. A more devoted, loving individual it would be hard to find - exactly as my brother had been, before he descended into poverty and took to the bottle. What I fear, is that his mounting debts and overriding material desires are clouding his judgement. Mrs Aston-Cowper is a wealthy woman, who is no doubt flattered by the attentions of a younger man. As such, they both have something to gain from the union. And yet, I fear it will be a marriage of simple convenience that one or both parties will live to regret."

"Watson, you have the upper hand on me. I feel disinclined to venture any opinion on Christopher's romantic inclinations and cannot claim to know his wider motivations. But what of the lady herself – what more do you know of her?"

"Alas, very little. I made some discreet enquiries at one of my dining clubs. A steward there knows of her, and furnished me with a few particulars. She is the widow of Sir Ashley Aston-Cowper, the eminent anatomist, famed for carrying out some pioneering arterial surgery on one of the Queen's continental cousins. When he passed away in February of last year, he left his wife a fashionable and expensive home in Bexley and a tidy annual income to match. Inexplicably, she has, since that time, ceased to use the honorific title of 'Lady Aston-Cowper'."

"Yes, indeed. But there is something more. I cannot recollect all of the details, but seem to remember that she was embroiled in some sort of scandal involving the younger son of the Duke of Buckland."

"Well, that is news to me!" I spluttered. "And what was the nature of this impropriety?"

"Given the delicacy of the situation, Watson, I am loath to tell you anything that is not completely accurate. I suggest we retrace our steps back to Baker Street, where I can consult my files and tell you all of the pertinent facts surrounding the *Cheddington Park Scandal*.

************************

The two-mile walk back to Baker Street lifted my mood considerably and I felt reassured that I had, at last, confided in Holmes. But at the back of my mind, I was now anxious that the matters he had referred to might exacerbate my woes about the marriage.

On entering 221B, we were greeted immediately by an agitated Mrs Hudson. "I'm so sorry, Mr Holmes, but the lady insisted on waiting for your return. I have just taken her a cup of tea, but she seems very emotional and has already sat upstairs for the best part of an hour."

"Understood, Mrs Hudson, then we will delay her no longer," Holmes replied, removing his overcoat and hat and nodding for me to do the same. "But do please tell us – who is our resolute, yet excitable guest?"

Mrs Hudson's reply came as a surprise to us both. "Her calling card says 'Aston-Cowper'...'Mrs Virginia Belvedere Aston-Cowper'."

We climbed the seventeen steps to the upstairs room and entered the study. Mrs Aston-Cowper stood promptly to greet us, dropping her small handbag on to the chair she had been sitting in. It was clear that she had been crying and she still held within her delicate, gloved left hand a small handkerchief which I gathered she had been using to dry her tears.

The lady appeared to be considerably younger than I had expected. While I knew her to be just over forty years of age, I could not in all honesty say that she looked a day over thirty. She was slender in build and around five feet, ten inches tall. Beneath her heavy black shawl, she wore a long, exquisitely tailored dress of green silk, which accentuated her slim figure. Her bright, delicate face was framed with a mass of dark curls, on which sat a velvet bonnet festooned with a colourful assembly of flowers. As I approached her, I was transfixed by her intense blue eyes.

Holmes greeted her warmly. "Mrs Aston-Cowper! I am so sorry to have kept you waiting." She raised her right hand towards him and he shook it gently. "I am Sherlock Holmes, as you may have guessed, and this is my colleague, Dr John Watson, the man you have really come to see. Please, be seated."

Her face took on a look of gentle surprise and she smiled pleasantly as I too shook the hand that was extended towards me. She then sat back down and proceeded to remove her shawl, black gloves and the green velvet bonnet, revealing the full extent of her brunette locks. "I suppose I should have guessed that a celebrated consulting detective would have little trouble in discerning the primary reason for my visit," she said, in a confident tone.

We both took seats facing her and I could not resist the opportunity to make an immediate observation: "Mrs Aston-Cowper, no doubt you wish to talk to me about your forthcoming marriage to my nephew Christopher? I imagine that he asked you to come here, knowing that if he had come himself, I would have expressed my displeasure at his hasty matrimonial plans. You may view me as overly-protective and unreasonably paternalistic towards him, but I think I should point out that Christopher is, in many respects, the closest thing I have to a son of my own. I have no reason to question your affections for him, but fear that he may be marrying you for his own selfish reasons."

Her response was both earnest and considered. "Dr Watson, I thank you for your honesty and directness, as I much prefer a man who says what is on his mind. Christopher knows nothing of my visit today. He holds you in high regard and has told me much about your loyalty and steadfast support for him and his studies. I have taken on the task of arranging all of the preparations for the wedding in order that Christopher may concentrate on the final batch of his university examinations. Of all the invitations I had sent out, yours was the only one which had not prompted any sort of reply. I am told that you are a proactive man, with a military disposition to get things done, so could envisage only two reasons for this. Either, you had not received the letter, or, having taken delivery of it, you had decided that you did not wish to attend the ceremony. My visit today was designed, in part, to clarify if the latter was the case and I recognise now that it was. I know how hurt Christopher will be if you are absent on the day, so I implore you to reconsider, for both our sakes."

I could not fail to be moved by her appeal and apologised for having not replied to the invitation. At that same time, I resisted the temptation to glance at Holmes, and wondered what he must be making of all this. I then found myself agreeing to attend the wedding, which elicited a most radiant smile from our guest.

"I am so happy to hear you say that, sir! And please, rest assured, I have the measure of Christopher and his wayward habits. Since we first met two months ago at a charitable event in Oxford, we have been the closest of kindred spirits and have both determined that there should be no secrets between us. I have been candid in telling him about my first marriage to Sir Ashley Aston-Cowper and some of the incidents in my life of which I am less than proud. He, likewise, has been open in sharing with me his addiction to gambling and his dishonesty in approaching many of his family and friends for funds to support his compulsion..."

Holmes shuffled in his chair and stifled a chortle with the pretence of a cough.

"...I am convinced now that he has put all of that behind him and is genuinely determined to complete his studies and take up a position he has been offered at Guy's Hospital."

I could but marvel at the turnaround in my nephew's fortunes if what I had heard was true. Having now met his intended and listened to her passionate defence of him, I hoped that this was indeed the case. I turned to the question of his career prospects - "And you say he has been approached by Guy's?"

"Yes, well, *approached* may not be an accurate interpretation. I will be honest in sharing with you that it was I that secured the offer. My late husband was very well regarded in his surgical role at Guy's and I have maintained close friendships with some of his former colleagues. It was not difficult to put in a good word for Christopher, knowing that he has both the skills and determination to succeed in his career."

This time it was Holmes who spoke. "It seems you have taken an extraordinary risk in placing your faith and love in a young man you have known for such a short time and who has yet to establish himself in society. You are a woman with both status and wealth. Are you not concerned that others may judge your betrothal to be reckless?"

"I have ceased to worry about what others may think. Call it an affectation of age, but I have reached a point in life where I choose to do those things which *feel* right, rather than those which are deemed by others to be the most rational or sensible course. Knowing something of your professional approach, Mr Holmes, I imagine that may be anathema to you."

My admiration for this woman was growing steadily and I could understand now why my nephew had become so infatuated with her. Undoubtedly, she had the measure of most of the men she encountered.

Holmes ignored her passing remark and changed tack, as only he could. "Mrs Aston-Cowper, it seems you have resolved the matter of Watson's attendance at your wedding. Perhaps now you will turn to the other pressing issue which has brought you here today. If I am not mistaken, you are seeking my help on the delicate matter of the *Cheddington Park Scandal*.

The lady was quite taken aback. She looked to me fleetingly, possibly seeking some sort of explanation or reassurance, but then turned her gaze back to Holmes, her penetrating blue eyes fixed on his. "That is most remarkable. How could you possibly know that?"

"Aligning a few facts and observations into a feasible hypothesis is the very essence of my craft – the science of deduction. Your earlier comments suggested that beyond the immediate matter of the wedding, you had a further, *secondary* reason for travelling across to Baker Street. This was clearly an issue of some importance, for you were prepared to wait over an hour for our return. And yet, you had not thought to send a telegram or to alert us in any other way to your impending visit. That this is also a very personal matter is evident from your emotional state. Putting both facts together suggests to me that something has happened very recently which has made this a more immediate concern, which you feel unable to deal with on your own. Perhaps there was also a degree of opportunism in coming here, knowing that your visit to Dr Watson might also provide you with access to his colleague, the detective. I am also aware that last year you were embroiled in some delicate matters at your Cheddington Park home, which may now have ramifications for the planned wedding. All in all, it seemed most likely that that would be the topic on which you would wish to consult me."

She continued to look at him in astonishment. "I declare that I am rarely shocked by much these days, Mr Holmes, but that has certainly caught me by surprise. I hope you will be able to assist me, but fear that I may be clutching at straws, as this is a most delicate and intractable problem. I would, of course, be pleased to reward you handsomely for any help you can provide..."

Holmes looked troubled by the reference to money and was quick to interject. "My dear lady, you need not concern yourself with the latter. I ask only that you acquaint me with the relevant facts of the case, so I may determine if there is any way that I can assist. Without the data, I can do nothing."

Mrs Aston-Cowper appeared to take this as a positive signal and offered up another of her beguiling smiles. "I will, then, begin at the very start and tell you all that I can. I am not sure how much will be relevant, but will let you decide the matters of substance. You will then understand why it is such a personal and immediate concern."

I took the opportunity to ask a quick question: "You have indicated that this is a very personal matter. Would you prefer it, if I were to leave at this point?"

"Certainly not, Doctor. I know that you work in close collaboration with Mr Holmes and can be trusted to be discreet. You have thus far been very open and honest with me. It is fitting that I should extend you the same courtesy."

I smiled and nodded. Holmes brought his fingertips together and raised them to his chin. He then planted his elbows on the arms of his chair and closed his eyes. Mrs Aston-Cowper then began her narrative.

\*\*\*\*\*\*\*\*\*\*\*\*\*\*\*\*\*\*\*\*\*\*\*

"My story begins in the summer of 1863, when I was just nineteen years old. My parents, Henry and Vivienne Melrose, felt strongly that all four of their female progeny should experience as much of life as was possible before marrying well and settling down to a quiet life of domesticity. Central to this enlightened ethos was the belief that travel would broaden our horizons and enrich our conversation. I had no great desire to travel, but faced with the gentle encouragement of my mother and the generous financial backing of my father, found myself that year in the colourful city of Paris. All of the arrangements had been made for me to stay for a period of six weeks, to see all that the metropolis had to offer and to make good use of the conversational French I had been learning for about a year. Travelling with me was Mrs Rose Sutherland, a seventy-year-old chaperone chosen by my mother, who had earlier accompanied my three older siblings to their favoured destinations in other parts of Europe.

"From the outset, the carefully formulated plans of my sojourn began to unravel, when dear Mrs Sutherland contracted a debilitating stomach complaint on the sea crossing to France and then spent the first week of the trip confined to her bed within the Hôtel de Crillon. I was content to amuse myself in and around the hotel while she recuperated, each day gaining the confidence to walk a little further from my base, seeking out whatever cultural diversions I could find. Of course, I told Mrs Sutherland nothing of these little excursions.

"On my third day, I visited the impressive gothic cathedral of Notre-Dame, and while walking close to the River Seine chanced upon a group of English artists painting an exterior view of the building. The party had travelled across to France together - a mixed group of male and female painters of all ages who seemed to revel in the relaxed bohemian atmosphere that Paris afforded them. My eye was drawn, in particular, to a watercolour by one of the older men, Gerald Stanhope, who told me that he was a student of the Royal Academy. Imagining that the picture would make a perfect gift for my parents, I asked him politely if it was for sale. He smiled and said that while he could not possibly take any money from me, he would be prepared to let me have the painting if I agreed to sit for him the next day.

"You will no doubt think me naïve, gentlemen, when I say that the proposition - put to me as it was on that fine, sunny day, along a beautiful stretch of river and among a group of talented artists – did not at the time strike me as odd or offensive. I agreed to meet up with the very charming Stanhope the next day, in the Pigalle garret he had rented for the duration of his stay. The following afternoon, I found my way to the garret and climbed the stairs to what was a small, but luxurious attic complex with access to a rooftop terrace overlooking the city's fine skyline. Stanhope had been true to his word and already had the watercolour wrapped for me to take away. That left the small matter of the sitting.

"Looking around the garret, I could see that he had been extremely industrious in his work; the walls, floor, tables and sofas of the apartment were covered in sketches, watercolours and canvases of all sizes. I could also see various bits of equipment which Stanhope informed me he had acquired for his developing interest in amateur photography. But the two small canvasses which really caught my attention were those hanging in pride of place on the wall of the main room. Both were of young women no older than myself, and each had been captured reclining and naked. I felt myself flush in embarrassment as I realised that this was what the artist now had in mind for me. With the bargain struck, I was immature enough to believe that I had no alternative but to go through with the sitting.

"I should say at this stage, that Stanhope acted without any hint of impropriety, busying himself with the easel and canvas and selecting his oil paints, as I began to remove my clothes. I thought only of the classical tradition of creative muses and the many women before me who had bared themselves in the name of art. It all felt very wrong, but I convinced myself mentally that it would all soon be over and no lasting harm would result. The artist then directed me to recline on the chaise longue he had prepared and which I recognised from the two paintings on the wall.

"Little by way of conversation passed between us, as he seemed to prefer to work without interruption and with an intensity of concentration that I had rarely seen in a fellow human being. The one concession I did extract from him was that in naming the finished painting, he was not to make any specific reference to the identity of the artist's model. This he agreed to happily, pointing out that he had already done that with his two earlier models. In any case, throughout the short time that I had known him, I had only ever referred to myself as 'Virginia'.

"Time passed very slowly in that cramped garret and within a couple of hours I announced that I would have to get dressed and make my way back to the hotel, as my elderly chaperone would, without doubt, be wondering where I was. As ever, Stanhope was friendly and obliging, but indicated that he was far from finished and would have to carry on the following day, expecting clearly that I would make a return visit. Realising this to be the case, my emotions got the better of me and the tears welled up within my eyes. He could see my obvious distress and suggested an alternative, which in the awkwardness of the moment seemed to be preferable. He would set up his camera and take a single photograph of me, from which he could then work at his leisure without any further imposition on me.

"That then was that. When I arrived back at the hotel, I found that Mrs Sutherland had barely missed me. I vowed never to tell a soul about the incident and believed that no one could possibly know what I had done. I realised, of course, that in my haste to get away from that claustrophobic apartment, I had not even paused to look at how Stanhope had portrayed me. Had I done so, I may not have been so confident that this was the end of the matter.

"There is little more to say about the Parisian trip beyond that. Mrs Sutherland failed to return to full health after that first week and we concluded that our best course of action would be to return home early. Over time, I put the whole affair out of my mind and it would only re-enter my thoughts when I glanced occasionally at the Notre-Dame watercolour that graced the wall of my parents' conservatory.

"When I was twenty-five, I met and fell in love with Sir Ashley Aston-Cowper, a distinguished medical man, some years older than me. We were not to be blessed with children and despite his status as a surgeon he suffered with persistent heart problems, exacerbated by his extravagant lifestyle and love of fine wine and rich food. Ours was a happy marriage for the most part, although we had distinctly different circles of friends with whom we spent time, when not together. My preference was to visit my parents and sisters. Sir Ashley liked to mix with the more elite and wealthy members of his various clubs, societies and medical institutions. Occasionally, he would invite some of these to stay for the weekend in the exterior lodge close to the entrance of our Cheddington Park home. It was during this time that I first became acquainted with Roger Morton, the youngest son of the Duke of Buckland.

"From the outset, I disliked the man intensely. He was close to my own age, and younger than most of the group that my husband entertained on a regular basis. In short, he was brash, uncouth and self-obsessed. But what I particularly detested, were his barely concealed attempts to flirt with me in the presence of my husband. Sir Ashley seemed not to notice and clearly saw something in the man that eluded me. Morton lived off the not insignificant allowance that he received from his father, but maintained that he was an art dealer. And it was in this capacity, that he was to bring the past back to haunt me.

"Sir Ashley had invited a dozen guests over one weekend in February last year. Morton had arrived ahead of the others and seemed particularly pleased with himself, saying - out of earshot of my husband - that he had a surprise for me. He explained that the previous week he had purchased a job lot of paintings and ephemera from a major dealer in Brussels. This had included a number of works by British artists, including 'Gerald Stanhope'. He paused, allowing the name to hang in the air and watching for my reaction. I froze instantly, in the dawning realisation of what he had just said, and felt a cold chill descend through my body. 'So, it is you in the painting - I guessed as much!' he whispered with a smirk, before following one of our servants who was carrying Morton's bags and cases in through the door of the lodge.

"I recognised that Morton had the upper hand and the future of my marriage, if not my standing in society generally, would indeed be precarious if he were to reveal the painting to anyone. That Friday evening he seemed content to let the matter rest, casting me lascivious looks every time our eyes met. And it was only before lunchtime the following day that his intentions became clear. Catching me in the grounds of the house as I strolled through my favourite rose garden, Morton took me by the arm and announced that he wanted me as his mistress. He then added that if I were to refuse, he would reveal the painting to our guests that very evening. He left me to think it over.

"In that instant, I determined that I would not be held to ransom by the scoundrel and realised one immediate fact. Namely, that in threatening me, he had clearly brought the canvas with him. If I could find a way to get to the picture and destroy it, my future might yet be saved. As luck would have it, Sir Ashley had provided me with a perfect opportunity to put my plan into action. Over lunch, he announced that all of the guests were invited to take part in a bridge tournament in the main house, a proposal that all agreed to readily.

"That afternoon, feigning a headache, I left our guests to their card playing and headed for the kitchen, where I took from one of the cutlery drawers a small, sharpened fruit knife, which I hoped would be sufficient to cut the canvas from its frame. I then took a side door from the house, out of sight of the servants, and walked the short distance down the drive to the lodge. With all of the guests being entertained at the main house, I knew that the lodge would be deserted.

"When I entered Morton's room, I could see no obvious place in which he could have hidden the painting. All of the bags and cases he had brought with him were empty, their original contents having been placed in the drawers and wardrobe of the bedroom. That left only the small loft space above the bed. I retrieved a set of wooden steps from an adjoining room and climbed until I was able to push open the loft door and look inside. To my frustration, I could see nothing in the darkness and had to come back down the ladder to find a hurricane lantern in a store cupboard, which I lit to take back up with me. My second attempt met with success as I could now see, some five feet from my grasp, a wrapped package which I guessed to be the canvas. But as I went to climb further up the ladder and into the loft, I felt a rough tug on my left ankle and heard Morton shout loudly for me to come down. Startled, I lost control of the lantern and it fell heavily, the glass globe breaking and igniting the paraffin which spilled out from the lamp.

"Morton dragged me bodily from the ladder and pushed me aside before climbing on the steps and trying to ascend into

23

the loft. I seized the opportunity and ran from the room as he was driven back by the flames now engulfing the tinder dry rafters of the roof space. When I managed to get back to the safety of the house, I raised the alarm and soon both servants and guests were running to and from the lodge with buckets of water in a futile attempt to extinguish the inferno.

"Sir Ashley knew that at the time of the fire only Morton and I had been at the lodge. Morton had dropped out of the card game early on, saying that he needed to retrieve something from the lodge. Having raced back to the house to raise the alarm, it was obvious that I had not been in my room suffering with a headache. That evening, with the lodge now completely devastated by the fire, my husband called both Morton and I to his study and asked for an explanation. My initial fear was that our guest would now take his revenge by telling Sir Ashley all about the painting, which had also been destroyed. However, he went one step further in his vengeance, claiming that we had been having a secret affair for months and I had talked about the prospect of marriage once Sir Ashley had succumbed to the inevitable heart disease with which he was afflicted.

"I need hardly tell you, Mr Holmes, that what Morton did that evening was far worse than revealing the existence of a scandalous painting. When Sir Ashley looked at me for some challenge or corroboration of the story, I fell mute – unable to defend myself or tell him what had really gone on. Morton was told in no uncertain terms to leave Cheddington Park immediately and to never show his face in front of Sir Ashley again. I was instructed that while we would give outsiders and household staff the impression that our marriage was solid we would, from that moment on, cease to be husband and wife. In the event, there was no need for any such pretence. The shock of the alleged affair was more than my husband's heart could take and during the night he suffered a fatal attack.

"Of course, with a house full of well-connected guests whose weekend had been cut short by the drama of what had gone on, it did not take long for the rumours to start circulating. A mysterious fire, the unexpected death of a Knight and talk that his Lady wife had been having an affair were bound to have a resonance. Some of Sir Ashley's friends and colleagues began to shun me, but on the whole most were supportive in my hour of need. Most significantly, Roger Morton seemed to have disappeared and I was told later by one of our circle that he had gone to New York to work for an auction house.

"The fact that the provisions of Sir Ashley's will remained unchanged and I was left both Cheddington Park and an annual income helped to persuade some doubters that there had been no obvious rift between the two of us. But I felt distinctly uncomfortable about the bequest and decided to cease using the title 'Lady Aston-Cowper'. It was a small gesture, but it was my way of showing that I did not want to dishonour the memory of my dear husband.

"After some months, my life began to return to some semblance of normality, helped by the unerring support of my family. And, most recently, I met Christopher, who has proved to be the most loyal and compassionate man I have ever known. As we became closer, I took the decision to share with him the full story of what the newspapers had called the *Cheddington Park Scandal*."

Our guest paused briefly, and Holmes – who had to that point given every impression of being fast asleep – opened his eyes quizzically, and prompted our guest: "Please, Mrs Aston-Cowper, I think you were about to bring us up to date and reveal the telegram you received this morning from Roger

Morton threatening to make public the photograph taken of you by Gerald Stanhope."

The lady swallowed heavily. "Yes, indeed, Mr Holmes, but I am again in awe of your deductive capabilities. I made no mention of the telegram..."

"No. But you did not challenge me when I put it to you earlier that something had happened very recently. And when we entered the room it was clear that you had been re-reading something which had once again brought you to tears. For reasons of vanity, you were quick to dispense with the pince-nez which you slid swiftly into your chatelaine bag. The telegram did not fare so well – it still sits beside you, now looking rather crumpled, but clearly displaying today's date. As for the photograph, it struck me from your account that if Morton had managed to purchase Stanhope's original oil painting - and had been so sure that you were the model in it - it was also extremely likely that he had acquired the accompanying photograph. In my experience, blackmailers relish a solid back-up plan."

"Simply astonishing!" she uttered, a broad smile now covering her face. "So, vanity was my undoing, yet again. And you are quite correct about the content of the telegram. I had not heard one word from Roger Morton since the night of the fire and believed that he had no further hold on me with the destruction of the canvas. The telegram came as a complete shock."

"It would be helpful to see the precise wording of the message," said Holmes.

She rose from her chair and passed the telegram to my colleague. He looked it over for some minutes and then read aloud: *'More to come on Cheddington scandal...a photograph...will prevent marriage = M.'* Very interesting -

it seems that Mr Morton is determined to scupper your wedding plans, Mrs Aston-Cowper, and is prepared to go to great lengths to do so. That recent announcement in *The Times* has clearly been picked up by our man in America who now plans to travel back to England to sow the seeds of your undoing."

I then interposed. "Why do you say that, Holmes?"

"Well, he has no way of knowing that Mrs Aston-Cowper has already told your nephew about the canvas and photograph so is labouring under the delusion that his disclosure of the latter would prevent the wedding. That said, if the photograph were to fall into the wrong hands, it could still be tremendously damaging to both their reputations. And yet, Morton clings to some hope that he can negotiate a deal. If that were not the case, he would already have exposed the photograph to the American press, who would no doubt relish a story about the fall from grace of a British Lady. The telegram was sent from New York yesterday evening by the Western Union Telegraph Company. It seems to me that Morton despatched it before boarding a passenger liner for the transatlantic passage to Liverpool."

With that, he leapt from his seat and began to rummage through a pile of loose folders in a corner of the room. Mrs Aston-Cowper looked on with some consternation. When he returned to his seat a minute or two later, Holmes was waving a bright-coloured pamphlet.

"Here it is - a brochure for the British and North American Royal Mail Steam-Packet Company. The passenger liner *Scotia* was due to set off yesterday for the eastbound crossing. This is the oceangoing steamer that won the *Blue Riband* for the westbound passage three years ago. The voyage is estimated to take between ten and fourteen days, which should mean that Roger Morton will be docking at Liverpool in early September."

Mrs Aston-Cowper continued to look confused. "And what happens then?"

"Why, it should be a simple matter of greeting him at the port and persuading him to hand over the photograph," Holmes retorted. "That is a task you can leave to the inestimable talents of Dr Watson here."

I was flattered by Holmes faith in me, but not a little disturbed at the thought that the social standing of both my nephew and his bride to be might depend on my success in completing the mission. Mrs Aston-Cowper seemed delighted by the plan, rising from her chair to come and shake me warmly by the hand, before offering some words of encouragement.

"Doctor, I will forever be in your debt if you can manage to resolve this issue. It is more than I could have hoped for in coming here today, when my principal objective was to persuade you to attend a wedding! And I will be eternally grateful for the professional assistance you have offered, Mr Holmes. You have a rare set of talents. I must now take my leave. And while I am loath to keep anything from Christopher - as I hinted at earlier - I do believe it would be better for all concerned, if nothing more was said about our meeting today."

"That would be best for us all," agreed Holmes, with a mischievous smile. "Without any disrespect to you, Mrs Aston-Cowper, I would not wish it to be known by my colleagues at Scotland Yard that I am now providing guidance on marital matters."

Our client left us in good humour and I looked forward to meeting her again at the wedding that October. For the next week or so, I sought regular updates from the steamship company on the likely progress of the *Scotia* and made plans to travel up to the Port of Liverpool to greet the arrival of the passenger liner. When it berthed at the Albert Dock on Monday, 3rd September, I was more than prepared for the encounter with Roger Morton.

He emerged from the dock office in the company of a porter who was pulling a hand trolley on which sat a large cabin trunk. Morton was well over six-feet tall and solidly built. He was dressed in a knee-length tweed frock coat, a white shirt and wide dark-red necktie. On his head sat a tall top hat. He looked every part the English aristocrat.

As I stepped forward, he pre-empted my challenge. "Dr Watson, I take it? I understand that you are here to collect this from me," said he, thrusting a large envelope into my hand. There was no warmth in his tone and his dark brown eyes fixed on mine with a degree of menace. Not to be intimidated, I continued to hold his stare and then turned my attention to the envelope. As I opened it, I could see that it contained the salacious image of the young Virginia Melrose.

"Our business is concluded then, Mr Morton," I said, turning briskly and walking away to be bemused looks of the porter.

It was clear that Morton felt he had to have the last word. "For what it's worth, you can tell her that she was never a great beauty!" His words echoed around the dock office. I carried on walking.

When I arrived back at Baker Street a couple of days later, Holmes was waiting for me with a stiff glass of brandy. "Warm yourself up with this, Watson, it is unseasonably cold today."

I could not resist chiding him for the unnecessary display. "Holmes, I have known you too long to be fooled by any of this. You knew full well that Morton could be persuaded to hand over the letter. When I met him at the docks he already knew who is was. So, how did you do it?"

Holmes smirked, knowing that I was more relieved than upset by his intervention. "My dear fellow, I could not send you into battle without providing you with reinforcements. A quick visit to my brother Mycroft was all that was required. Having heard the story, he travelled up to Liverpool ahead of you and arranged to be taken out by tug to the *Scotia* as the liner began its entry to the port. When he tracked Morton down on board the ship, he made it clear that if the rogue did not hand the photograph to you at the dockside, both he and his father, the Duke of Buckland, would be blackballed in every gentleman's club in London. Furthermore, the Duke's loans on the current refurbishment of his Highland estates would be called in, rendering the family bankrupt. I suspect that was sufficient to seal the matter."

I was warmed by the subterfuge. "Then that is an end to the matter, Holmes. A job well done - I have destroyed the photograph, Mrs Aston-Cowper can rest easy, and we can all enjoy the wedding. Let's drink to that!"

# 2. The Curious Matter of the Missing Pearmain

"Splendid!" exclaimed Holmes suddenly, looking over a piece that had caught his eye in the *Daily Telegraph*. It was a chilly, yet bright, early morning in December 1894. My colleague had asked me to call on him first thing, as he said he had a new case that required my assistance. On arriving at Baker Street, I had been offered one of Mrs Hudson's marvellous cooked breakfasts and when seated upstairs beside my colleague, had eagerly partaken of the thickly-sliced bacon, fried egg, tomatoes and kedgeree that had been presented to me. In contrast, Holmes had contented himself with a single piece of toast and a strong black coffee and had remained largely uncommunicative beyond his initial greeting when I first entered the room.

He was dressed in a long crimson dressing gown, under which I could see that he was already prepared for a formal engagement of some kind. Beneath the open silk gown he was wearing some sharply-pleated grey pinstripe trousers, white cloth spats, a starched dress shirt and a black bow-tie. I had already noted the black frock-coat which Mrs Hudson had placed on a hanger to his left and the top hat which Holmes had positioned, somewhat incongruously, on the head of a plaster death mask, which sat in pride of place on the mantelpiece.

"What is 'splendid', Holmes?" I queried, with obvious irritation, having waited for further words or some suitable explanation which had not been forthcoming.

Holmes seemed impervious to my agitation. "It seems that Inspector Lestrade has a rare murder mystery for us to consider, Watson. I apologise for not having explained matters more fully in my earlier telegram, but I need you to meet with the good inspector when he arrives here at nine o'clock this morning. This piece in the *Daily Telegraph* gives us some indication of the puzzle which Lestrade is faced with and the reason he is so keen to seek my assistance."

I resisted the temptation to ask him about the newspaper article and went straight to the crux of the matter: "So, you've called me here to meet with Lestrade at the appointed time, so that you are free to swan off to some prior engagement. Well, I must say, Holmes, I find this most irregular. While my medical practice is quiet at the present time, you know that I am not without commitments, engagements and responsibilities of my own."

Holmes seemed genuinely stunned by my rebuke and a look of concern crept over his pallid-white features. "My dear Watson, it seems I have been very thoughtless in taking your assistance for granted and presuming that you would be able to stand in for me. I meant no offence, but believe this will be an affair worthy of our attention, since it will be the first time that we have heard from Lestrade since April of this year, when we were involved in what you described, very commendably, in your published accounts as *The Adventure of the Empty House*."

Ever susceptible to my colleague's effortless flattery, I was determined to hold out a while longer. "That's all well and good, Holmes, but you haven't even told me what this other appointment is and why you cannot meet with Lestrade yourself."

"It is a small distraction, I assure you. I would much rather meet with our police colleague and had planned to do so when I responded to his request yesterday evening. However, about nine o'clock last night, I received a hasty and unexpected visit from my brother Mycroft. He informed me, rather belatedly, that I am required to attend a lunch appointment at the Danish Embassy today, at which I will be awarded the *Order of the Dannebrog*. I was told about the honour some weeks ago and had asked for it to be posted to me. Mycroft explained that I was likely to cause offence - and something of a diplomatic incident - if I continued along that path and persuaded me instead to accept the award in good faith from the King of Denmark, Christian IX, who is visiting London this week."

I could scarcely believe that Holmes had not thought to mention this news earlier and expressed my astonishment at his reticence. He explained that Danish protocol had prevented him from talking about the matter until the award had been received. "In any case," he added, "The honour was given for my very inconspicuous assistance in saving his youngest son, Valdemar, from some risky investment schemes which contributed to the collapse of a major commercial bank in Canada – an entanglement which would have resulted in considerable public scrutiny and financial ruin for the prince. The King has demanded that both the affair, and my role in resolving it, should be kept from the public gaze."

"Understood, Holmes, but you know that I could have been relied upon to be discreet. There was no need to act so furtively."

"I realise that now, but my primary concern was to ensure that Lestrade was not put off in coming to us with his case – he trusts and respects you as much as he does me. I need hardly tell you, that I would rather be presented with a single, intangible mental challenge to flatter and sustain my ego, than I would a dozen knighthoods. I seek stimulation not adulation."

Realising this to be the case and having no wish to continue to chastise my colleague, I turned my attention to the newspaper and asked Holmes to relay what had been printed in the *Daily Telegraph*. Having lit his favourite churchwarden and taken two or three puffs of the pipe, he read out the news item:

### *Mysterious Death at Ravensmere Towers*

*Detectives from Scotland Yard were called yesterday afternoon to the prestigious new office building of Ravensmere Towers near Hyde Park, following a report of a fatal shooting.*

*While details remain sketchy, our chief reporter understands that the incident is being treated as a potential case of murder, since no firearm was found near the body. The victim of the shooting was a Mr Edward J Flanagan, an Irish national, who occupied the first floor office of Ravensmere Towers, where he ran a successful business exporting English porcelain to the United States.*

*Detectives admit to being baffled by the circumstances of the death. The building is accessible only from the ground floor, the sealed entrance to which is controlled by a vigilant concierge. He has stated categorically that beyond those few personnel occupying the plush offices, no one entered or left the building during the time the shooting is believed to have taken place. However, when the Scotland Yard men, led by the very capable Inspector Lestrade, conducted a thorough search of the building, they were unable to find the illusive gunman.*

*The only other paying tenants of Ravensmere Towers are three brothers in their forties, who operate a depository for rare books on the second floor. They claim to have heard a single, very audible shot at around eleven o'clock yesterday morning. Some moments after this, Mr Chester Godbold - the eldest of the trio - ventured out of their rooms in order to determine the source of the noise. Having done so, he claims to have caught a glimpse of a man holding a revolver, running up the stairs to the third floor. The man was said to be wearing a heavy grey overcoat and a large tweed hat which covered his head and the sides of his face and prevented Mr Godbold from seeing more of his features.*

*Inspector Lestrade was reluctant to say any more about the supposed crime at this juncture.*

*Readers may remember that Ravensmere Towers was opened at the start of this year to some fanfare. It is said to be one of the most impressive modern buildings in the capital. Its offices are fully-equipped with electric lighting and power and all upper floors are accessible via a hydraulic-powered lift, or elevator, in addition to a traditional stairwell. The owner and property developer, Mr Archibald Cartwright, occupies the third floor of the building, and was said to be 'deeply saddened' by the events and has pledged to do all he can to assist the police in bringing to justice the man responsible for the shooting.*

"Well, what do you make of it, Watson?" queried Holmes, placing the open newspaper on the table in front of him.

"Quite remarkable. Lestrade and his men were unable to find any lone gunman, so unless the concierge is mistaken – or had, indeed, carried out the shooting himself – the assailant must have been one of those within the building at the time."

"A perfect summary, my friend. We will certainly need to ascertain whether the concierge can be trusted and whether he could have been mistaken about the apparent security of the building. Beyond that, it will be imperative to find out three things: firstly, some further information about the victim, this Mr Flanagan; secondly, full intelligence on the other occupants of the building and, crucially, where each was at the time of the shooting; and lastly, precise details of the layout and accessibility of the ground and five upper floors of Ravensmere Towers."

A large halo of grey smoke was caught momentarily in the sunlight that had begun to stream in through the large window of the study. Holmes stood and placed the churchwarden on the mantelpiece and lifted the top hat from the death mask, before adding: "Not an insubstantial task, I grant you, but one that I am confident you can achieve during my absence today."

Within a few minutes he was fully dressed and ready to depart. A prompt ring on the doorbell some moments later indicated that his carriage had arrived and with a cheery smile and a snappy wave of the hand, Holmes was off down the stairs for his appointment at the embassy. I watched from the window as the Hansom cab departed and then returned to my chair to prepare a long list of questions for Inspector Lestrade.

***********************

The doughty inspector arrived some fifty minutes later and was visibly dejected and decidedly unimpressed when told that Holmes had departed for a hastily arranged appointment with a European royal. His pinched and drawn features and deep, hollow-set eyes took on a most unusual expression as he pondered how he might proceed in the light of the news. He then sat in the armchair that Holmes had vacated earlier.

"Well, I suppose I can convey to you the key facts as we know them, Dr Watson. You are familiar with Mr Holmes' methods I dare say, so you can prompt me if I fail to explain all of the finer details." He then glanced across at the *Daily Telegraph* which still sat on the table. "I see that you have already read a little of the case."

"Yes indeed, Inspector, but I would prefer to hear your first-hand account of what you discovered at Ravensmere Towers. Holmes was most insistent that I obtain all of the relevant particulars, so that he may assist you when he returns to Baker Street later this afternoon."

Lestrade's demeanour was transformed instantly on hearing this. His face brightened and he at once sat upright in the chair and started to recount what had occurred the previous day. For my part, I began to take copious notes of everything the inspector presented.

"Well, we arrived at Ravensmere Towers close to midday – my good self and two uniformed constables. The telegram requesting our assistance had been sent by the secretary of Archibald Cartwright, the owner of the building. He greeted us at the door and introduced us to the concierge, James Mount, who then escorted us around the building for the duration of our stay. I insisted that he lock the entrance at that point, to allow no one to leave the building."

"And could you describe the layout of the ground floor, Inspector?"

"Fairly straightforward. The main entrance consists of two large doors. Anyone wishing to enter Ravensmere Towers must pull a cord outside the building to ring a large internal bell. They are then afforded an entrance by Mr Mount. He has a reception desk and small office just inside the doors with a window looking out onto the street. In that way, he is able to view any entrants before admitting them. During the day, one of the doors is kept on a latch. It is possible to open the latch from the inside and get out of the building, but it cannot be opened from the outside. During the night, both doors are securely locked with keys held by the concierge, who is always the last to leave the building.

"The main part of the space is taken up with two washrooms which have been installed for all of the office workers - one for the ladies and the other for the gentlemen of the building. They contain toilet facilities and cloakrooms. The windows to these are covered in wrought-iron bars preventing any exit from the building. Outside of the washrooms, towards the centre of the lobby, is the main stairwell, which ascends to the five upper floors. At the heart of this, is the building's lift, or elevator, system. And very impressive it is too, Dr Watson."

"In what way?" I enquired, having little idea what the contraption consisted of.

"I was told by Mr Cartwright that this is the first office building in London to have such a machine. It is a square box, some eight or nine feet across. An iron gate at its entrance is slid across to allow the office workers to step into it. When the gate has been returned to its original position, those inside can operate a series of levers which then transport the box up to their desired floor." He paused at that point and withdrew his black police notebook from an inside pocket, before continuing to provide further minutiae.

"The contrivance is powered by water under pressure, which comes from a nearby hydraulic power station, which is itself driven by coal-fired steam engines. The whole system is delivered by the London Hydraulic Power Company, which operates north of the Thames. I confess that the details of how it works escape me, but it certainly takes the legwork out of climbing stairs in such a tall building."

"I can imagine, Inspector. It sounds like an incredible device. And can this lifting box be accessed from each floor of the building?"

"Yes, although it appears that Mr Cartwright makes the greatest use of it. The concierge accompanies any visitors to the building and also assists the secretary, Miss Trelawney, who travels in the lift each morning to get to her room on the third floor. The concierge told me that the noise of the mechanism terrifies the Godbold brothers on the second floor and the dead man, Mr Flanagan, preferred to use the stairs to get to his first floor office, as the lift is very slow to operate."

"I see. So that accounts for the ground floor. What about the rest of the building and its inhabitants?" I then asked.

"The body was found on the first floor. You will know something of Mr Flanagan from the newspaper account. The floor consists of two linked rooms which serve as one rented office. Access to both is through a single door which faces the stairwell and lift. The first room is windowless and contains a desk and some other office furniture. A further door at the rear leads to the second room, which the Irishman used as a storeroom for his valuable porcelain pieces."

"Two questions, Inspector. Firstly, was Flanagan in the habit of locking the door to his office when at work? And secondly, does the storeroom contain windows that can be opened?"

"The answers to both questions is 'No', Doctor. Flanagan locked the door each evening when he left the office. The concierge suggested that this was usually around five-thirty. But during the day, he kept the door unlocked and rarely left his rooms. The windows are a modern design and permanently fixed. They cannot be opened."

39

"Thank you, Lestrade. That is most clear. And what can you tell me about the body?"

"Flanagan appears to have been shot at close range, which suggests a handgun of some kind. But there was no weapon in the vicinity. The local doctor who arrived later to remove the body, said the death was most likely instantaneous and the result of the substantial blood loss from a single, fatal shot to the heart. He has agreed to let me know if his *post mortem* examination throws up any further information. Acting on the statement given by Chester Godbold, we searched all floors of the building but were unable to find the gunman."

"How odd," I suggested, "And you are inclined to trust the judgement of Mr Mount, that no one could have entered or left the building without his knowledge?"

Lestrade did not hesitate in his response: "I am, Doctor. James Mount could be said to have hidden his light under a bushel. While serving now as a very conscientious concierge, he was formerly in the Royal Horse Guards and has an exemplary military service record."

"And did he share with you any useful observations on the shooting or the character of Edward Flanagan?"

At this point, the Inspector paused, sat back in the armchair and took a deep breath before answering. "Now, it's strange that you should ask me that, because he did say something that struck me as irregular. He claimed that no one in the building actually liked Flanagan, whom he described as abrupt, obtuse and argumentative. Flanagan was the first tenant to take an office in Ravensmere Towers and acted like he owned the place. He had apparently fallen out with Chester, Arthur and Frederick Godbold when they first moved in, some two months ago – claiming that they were making too much noise moving around on the floor above him. Mount also said that Flanagan was a few months behind on his rent and had heard Cartwright threatening to evict him on more than one occasion. Only two days ago, Flanagan had also upset Miss Trelawney, the secretary, shouting at her when she refused to allow him in to see Cartwright to discuss the rent situation. All in all, Mount believed him to be a bit of a trouble maker."

Reflecting on the characters discussed thus far, I then sought some further clarification. "Inspector, you have mentioned Flanagan, the concierge, the Godbolds on floor two and Cartwright and his secretary on floor three. But were there any other tenants or visitors in the building that day?"

The answer was again simple and direct. "No, Doctor. That is our entire cast, with the exception of the missing assassin. And if you want my view on how he could have escaped, I would say that it must have been during those first few minutes when the concierge ran up the stairs in response to the shouting of Chester Godbold. Mount told me that when the shot was fired he was in his office and heard only a muffled bang. At first, he believed it had come from the street, but stepped outside the office to listen further. He thought he could hear someone running on the stairs, but could not tell if they were ascending or descending. And as he strained to hear more, was suddenly aware of the cries for help and ran up the stairs to be greeted by the three Godbold brothers in some distress. If our mystery assailant was hidden in one of the washrooms at that time, he could have made his exit from the building shortly afterwards, out of sight of the concierge, and pulling the latch to behind him."

From what I had heard, I could only concur with the meticulous detective. And seeing that Lestrade looked to be flagging somewhat, I suggested that we take a short break and enjoy a pot of tea and a slice of fruit cake which Mrs Hudson had very kindly prepared for us. For a short while, Lestrade chatted amiably about life at Scotland Yard and some of the other cases he was working on, but within fifteen minutes he had returned to the events at Ravensmere Towers.

"I ought to furnish you with some further information about the two remaining floors of Ravensmere Towers - I know that Mr Holmes is a stickler for detail. The first four upper floors are of a similar layout and design, with the two adjoining rooms being accessed from the main door facing the stairwell and lift area. All contain the same basic items of furniture and are let as furnished offices. The commonality of design extends to the large, potted plants which adorn each office and run down the walls to the left of each of the main office doors.

"Floor four also has a short corridor running from the back room – the one with windows – to a second door, which provides an alternative exit to the lift and stairwell. It sits to the left of the main office door, obscured by the line of potted plants. The top floor is different again, being but a single open office which runs around the lift and stairwell. Mr Cartwright explained that it was designed to be a large storage area for a business venture which needs only to make the most of the space available without any sort of reception area or desk. The room contains just two small filing cabinets."

"Well, that all seems straightforward, Lestrade. And is there anything further you can tell me about the Godbolds, Mr Cartwright and Miss Trelawney and where they all were when the fatal shot was fired?"

"The Godbolds are strange, but likeable enough. The book business seems to suit them, being studious, academic types. I would be surprised if any of them knew how to hold a handgun. They were petrified when I first questioned them – concerned that the killer was still at large in the building.

They claim that when the shot was fired, all three of them were in the back room of their office. Chester Godbold was prevailed upon to go out onto the stairwell and ascertain what had caused the explosion. And when he stepped outside the door, he saw the alleged gunman heading up the stairs. He called for help and was joined shortly afterwards by both his brothers and the concierge. When I questioned him later, he was unable to provide any details beyond the short description of the man you will have read in the newspaper.

"According to his account, James Mount then took charge of the proceedings. He told the Godbolds to stay where they were on the second floor while he ran down to the floor below. Having done so, he discovered Flanagan's body and realised that the porcelain dealer had been shot. As he could see no sign of a gun, he guessed that the shooter must still be in the building and searched the back room of Flanagan's office and then did a thorough search of the ground floor. But assuming my earlier theory to be correct, I imagine our killer had by then already left the building. Mount returned once more to the Godbolds and encouraged them to follow him down to the ground floor, where he felt they would all be safer. When they had assembled in the entrance lobby, they were concerned to hear that the lift had suddenly started to operate. The Godbolds were told to lock themselves in one of the washrooms, while Mount ran to his office and retrieved his old service revolver from a desk drawer. He was prepared for an encounter with the gunman, but when the lift had descended to the ground floor, he was relieved to see that it was occupied by Mr Cartwright and Miss Trelawney, who had left their office to find out why there was such a commotion elsewhere in the building."

I interrupted at this point. "So, Cartwright and Trelawney were in their third floor office when the shot was fired?"

"Yes, that would appear to be the case. When I spoke to her later, Miss Trelawney said that she had heard a bang, but the sound had been some way off and had not given her much cause for concern. It was only when Cartwright emerged from the back room some minutes later, expressing some anxiety about the noise that she began to view it more seriously. Cartwright suggested that they make their way down to the ground floor to consult with the concierge. He picked up her work tray on the way out and the pair then headed for the lift in order to reach the ground floor, where they were greeted by the sight of James Mount armed with his revolver. He apologised as they emerged from the lift and explained that Flanagan had been shot and it was his firm belief that the killer was still somewhere in the building. Cartwright insisted that they all stay together on the ground floor with the exception of Miss Trelawney, who was instructed to walk to the nearest post office in order to despatch a telegram to Scotland Yard requesting immediate assistance."

A small detail in Lestrade's account piqued my interest. "Why did Cartwright insist on picking up Miss Trelawney's work tray, Inspector? Did he elaborate at all?"

"Yes. He said that she had been working on some of his monthly accounts and the papers in the tray were highly confidential. He indicated that he didn't like the idea of leaving them behind in an unlocked office and thought it was easier and quicker to pick up the tray and take it with him, rather than spend time locking doors behind him."

"I see. And what have you found out about Cartwright and Trelawney - anything that might shed light on this curious incident?"

"Cartwright made no secret of the fact that he had been chasing Flanagan for his unpaid rent, but aside from that suggested that the two of them got along well enough. The

44

businessman made his fortune buying and selling commercial properties and has invested a considerable amount of capital in Ravensmere Towers. He strikes me as a determined and direct fellow who usually gets what he wants. He had no clear idea about who may have wished to shoot Flanagan, but admitted that the man had not been popular with the other office workers.

"Cartwright's secretary, Violet Trelawney, is twenty-two years of age and was taken on only recently. In fact, she has worked at Ravensmere Towers for less than a week. She was on the books of a secretarial agency before that, and was chosen by Cartwright from a shortlist of five candidates. He claims that she came with first rate credentials as a clerical worker and her references spoke highly of her character and, in particular, her integrity and reliability."

"You mentioned earlier that she had been upset by one of Flanagan's recent outbursts. Do you think that may have had some bearing on the events yesterday?" I queried.

"I don't think so. Miss Trelawney came across as a hard-working and honest young woman. She was upset by his abrupt manner, but said that she would not have wished him harm. There was, however, one small discrepancy in the statement that she gave to one of my constables."

I raised an eyebrow on hearing this. "And what was that?"

"Well, it is such a small and inconsequential matter that I am loath to make anything of it, but know how Mr Holmes insists on scrutinising the smallest of details. Asked if she could remember anything unusual about the events that morning, she told PC Clarke that when she had first sat down at her desk she had removed a Worcester Pearmain apple from her bag and placed it in the top drawer of her desk. She had intended to eat it later that morning and put it in the drawer,

45

out of sight, as Mr Cartwright had made it clear from her first day in the office that he did not wish to see any personal belongings left on the desk. She claimed it was a particular obsession of his and that any work she had been given was always placed in a simple wooden tray on the desk, for he would not allow her to have any other items on display."

I could see no particular mystery in this or, indeed, any obvious discrepancy with anything I had yet heard. Lestrade could see the concern on my face and went on to explain.

"Of itself, this does not sound very odd, I grant you. But the point I am getting to, is what Miss Trelawney went on to say. She claimed that when she returned to her desk later that afternoon - after we had completed a full search of the building and found no killer - the apple had disappeared from the desk. By my reckoning, there are only two possible explanations for that. Firstly, that she had been mistaken about the apple in the drawer, or, alternatively, that someone had taken it. And if the latter were the case, it could only have been taken by Cartwright or the killer. When I questioned him, Cartwright said he knew nothing about any apple and expressed some annoyance that my investigations should focus on such a triviality."

"Most strange," I replied, trying to hide my own feeling that this was indeed a piece of frippery in the overall scheme of events. Nevertheless, I recorded the relevant facts in my notes to share with Holmes later that day.

For the remainder of our time together, Lestrade explained how the case had been left. Having taken statements from all of the office staff, the police officers had allowed everyone to leave Ravensmere Towers and Lestrade had taken possession of all of the keys to the building. Cartwright had apparently voiced his opposition to this, but the inspector had been insistent. He said that his officers would complete their work

46

the following day and the keys would then be returned to the owner the day after. A constable had been left in the office of the concierge to ensure that no one entered the building without permission. In this way, Lestrade believed he had done all he could to preserve for Holmes whatever clues might still remain to be found. He ended by saying that he hoped my colleague would be able to get across to Ravensmere Towers in the late afternoon or early evening to assist with the investigation. I agreed to send a telegram to Lestrade when Holmes had returned and the inspector then departed, looking noticeably more chipper than when he had first arrived at Baker Street.

***********************

It was a little beyond four o'clock that afternoon when Holmes returned to Baker Street. For a man who had just been awarded a knighthood, he looked remarkably sombre and grumbled about the length of time it had taken to complete the ceremonial luncheon. It was all I could do to get him to open the small presentation box and show me the elaborate enamelled white cross he had been given by the king. With little further thought he placed it on the mantelpiece and picked up his pipe.

Having relit the churchman, Holmes sat in his favourite armchair and insisted that I run through the notes I had taken of my discussions with Lestrade. In a fog of tobacco smoke, I spent the next twenty minutes recounting all of the relevant facts while he sat cross-legged, listening intently to every word. When I had finished the recitation, Holmes was glowing in his praise for my note-taking.

"An excellent job, Watson! You have painted a very comprehensive picture of the events yesterday and given me a clear understanding of the facts as they stand. I have no doubt that we can assist Lestrade in resolving this matter later today. But there is no time to lose - I suggest you despatch your telegram immediately and inform the inspector that we will meet him at Ravensmere Towers around five-fifteen. And I would be grateful if you could ask him to request that Archibald Cartwright, Violet Trelawney, James Mount and the three Godbold brothers are also in attendance."

It took me but a short while to walk to the nearest post office and send the required telegram to Scotland Yard. When I returned to Baker Street, Holmes was already waiting outside in a carriage he had hailed to transport us the short distance to Hyde Park. At the appointed time, we stood on the pavement looking up at the impressive façade of Ravensmere Towers.

The building had been constructed in an Italianate style, with large pediment windows and neo-classical stone corbels beneath each projecting sill. The stonework had a gleaming white sheen, and two large, dark blue entrance doors complemented the front of the structure. At the corners of the roof line stood two short decorative towers which framed the building and added to its grandeur. It was clear that Archibald Cartwright had spent a significant amount of money on both the design and construction.

Holmes pulled the cord to the right of the entrance doors to ring the doorbell. Presently, we were admitted by a young police officer who introduced himself as PC Clarke. On entering the lobby of the ground floor we were greeted by Inspector Lestrade, a uniformed concierge and what I guessed to be our assembled party of office workers. Lestrade was effusive in his welcome.

"Mr Holmes, Dr Watson. Thank you both for turning out. I trust your journey was not too onerous?"

After some initial pleasantries and introductions, Holmes asked if James Mount could accompany him on a tour of the building. The concierge was eager to oblige and Lestrade passed to my colleague the set of keys which he had earlier taken charge of. After a couple of minutes examining the ground floor washrooms, Holmes asked if Mount could operate the office lift and take him to each floor of the building. Within minutes, the two men had disappeared from our view.

For the next half an hour Lestrade and I chatted amiably to the group. The auburn-haired Violet Trelawney seemed visibly animated by the proceedings and the three Godbold brothers overcame their initial reticence to talk openly and enthusiastically about the book trade. Only Cartwright remained impassive. When the lift returned once more to the ground floor, I could see from Holmes' expression that the tour had been productive. The glint in his eye was unmistakable.

"My dear Lestrade. That was most instructive. This lift, or elevator, is indeed a wonderful piece of machinery. I have just a few questions to ask Miss Trelawney before we progress any further."

With that, Holmes turned towards the young secretary and asked her to describe the sequence of events when she had first arrived at work the previous day. Violet Trelawney looked surprised by the request, but seemed content to take him through what she could recollect. In short, she had arrived at work at a quarter to nine and having deposited her coat and hat in the cloakroom of the ladies washroom, had emerged to find Mr Cartwright waiting for her at the entrance to the lift. She explained that on every other day in the office, it had been the concierge who had operated the lift and accompanied her to the third floor office where she worked.

When they were in the lift, Mr Cartwright had chatted to her about a musical performance he had seen the previous evening and seemed far more lively than usual. On reaching the office, he had unlocked the door to their rooms and she had taken a seat at her desk. She then waited for Mr Cartwright to go through to his room and return a short while later with the wooden tray which contained her work for the day. He gave instructions that he was not to be disturbed under any circumstances and had retreated into his room once more, closing the door behind him. This was the pattern that had been followed every day that Violet Trelawney had worked at Ravensmere Towers. Very occasionally, Mr Cartwright might emerge from his room with some additional requests, but, on the whole, the secretary was required to work diligently through her allotted work until one-thirty, when Mr Cartwright would come out from his room to announce the time and allow the young woman to go home for the day.

At this point, Holmes cut in. "Miss Trelawney, I think you have forgotten one small detail of the events yesterday. I understand that you placed an apple in your desk drawer?"

Miss Trelawney flushed. "Yes, I'm sorry, Mr Holmes. I had forgotten to mention that. When Mr Cartwright was in his office, I took the Worcester Pearmain from my bag and placed it in the drawer. When the police allowed me to return to the room in the afternoon, I found it had gone."

Archibald Cartwright scoffed loudly on hearing this and glowered at Holmes. "I might have thought that a consulting detective would have other, more pressing, matters to attend to, beyond a concern for *missing fruit*," he announced drily.

Holmes dealt with the challenge head on. "Sir, the absence of the apple lies at the very heart of this mystery as we will discover." Once more he turned his attention to Miss

Trelawney: "Perhaps you could explain what happened when you heard the shot at around eleven o'clock?"

"Yes. I heard the noise, but did not realise it was a gunshot until later. From where I sat, it was not particularly loud and I was a little surprised when Mr Cartwright came out of his room a good three or four minutes later, expressing some concern about it. He picked up my work tray and asked me to follow him to the lift, which we took to get to the ground floor where the others were then assembled. I was very upset to hear that Mr Flanagan had been shot."

"Indeed. And was there anything else that struck you as odd that morning?"

"Only one thing, Mr Holmes. I imagine it might be the drabness of the room in which I work, particularly with the absence of any windows or natural light, but I did at one point imagine that the walls were closing in on me. It made me feel quite giddy in fact."

Holmes smiled at her. "That is most enlightening, thank you. And a final question for you, Inspector Lestrade."

"Yes, Mr Holmes?"

"I understand you conducted a thorough search of the building when you first heard that the gunman had been seen ascending the stairs from the second floor?"

"That is correct. We looked in every room and checked every conceivable hiding place. The killer had clearly fled the building."

"And what if the killer had been one of the people already in the building – one of those now stood before us?"

There was considerable excitement at this point but Lestrade sought to quash the matter. "Mr Holmes, the killer cannot have been any of these good people. Each has a strong alibi and we could find no handgun on any of them. We searched every desk, drawer, cabinet and cupboard and found nothing to incriminate anybody."

"Ah, so you searched every room for the murder weapon?"

Lestrade looked confused. "Well, we conducted a detailed search of the ground floor and the first three upper floors, Mr Holmes. I admit that we undertook only a cursory exploration of floors four and five, principally to look for the killer - if we'd found him, we would have found the gun. There seemed little point searching any furniture on those floors as none of our suspects occupied the rooms."

"I see," said Holmes. "You will forgive me for pressing the point, but I just wanted to be clear. Now that you have given me that one final piece of the jigsaw, I am certain that I know how the murder was committed yesterday and who our killer is."

It was the Godbold brothers who were most voluble on hearing this and Violet Trelawney looked flabbergasted. Holmes then announced what was to be done. "If PC Clarke and Mr Mount are content to stand guard, I suggest that Inspector Lestrade and Miss Trelawney accompany Dr Watson and I in the lift to the third floor. I will then explain the sequence of events yesterday morning."

At this, Archibald Cartwright flared up and rounded on Holmes. "Sir, I refuse to be held captive in my own building! If you are suggesting that one of us committed this heinous crime, I insist that you provide us with the evidence for your assertions. Until such a time, I will not let you curtail my movements."

Holmes was unperturbed by Cartwright's outburst and extended him an invitation. "My dear fellow - I will be pleased to provide you with the proof you suggest. Perhaps you can stand in for Miss Trelawney on our short excursion. In fact, that would be a much better plan given that it was you that shot and killed Mr Edward J Flanagan."

There was not a little surprise at Holmes' announcement. Frederick Godbold, the youngest of the three brothers, swayed as if he was about to faint. Violet Trelawney looked close to tears and even Inspector Lestrade appeared to be astonished by the revelation. Of those present, it was Archibald Cartwright who remained the most composed of the group.

"Sir, you seem to be forgetting that I have a solid alibi for where I was at the time of the shooting. Miss Trelawney has confirmed that we arrived at the office together. Having given her a few tasks for completion, I withdrew to the back room. I only emerged from the room *after* I had heard the shot on the first floor. I think you will agree that if I had tried to leave the office by passing through Miss Trelawney's room, my secretary would, without doubt, have seen me."

Holmes reflected on Cartwright's words for a couple of seconds and then responded. "Yes, Mr Cartwright. There is a perfect logic to what you have said. And yet, it does not provide you with an alibi at all. I suggest that our party of four takes that trip to the third floor. All will become clearer as we travel up through the building."

Leaving the others in the lobby, Holmes and I escorted Lestrade and Cartwright towards the lift. We were safely ensconced within the elevator when Holmes began his narrative. "Gentlemen, Violet Trelawney was employed by Archibald Cartwright less than a week ago. Her excellent references spoke for her. He took her on because she was both hardworking and honest - not because he needed a secretary, but because she would provide him with an almost perfect alibi."

I could see Cartwright grinding his teeth, his jaw set hard and his eyes fixed firmly on the floor of the lift. Holmes operated a lever for the third floor and with a sudden jolt the mechanism was propelled into action, accompanied by a loud hiss and the noisy whirring of the machinery above and below us. I felt somewhat unnerved and momentarily dizzy as we began to ascend upwards.

Holmes raised his voice above the level of the clatter. "Miss Trelawney stated that when she emerged from the ladies washroom on the fateful morning, Mr Cartwright was waiting for her at the entrance to this lift. It is my contention that this was no coincidence. He planned it that way. It was essential that he take control of the lift and ensure that it was not the lever to their third floor office that was engaged, but the lever to the fourth floor instead. Miss Trelawney described him as being more lively than usual. His idle banter provided a cover for the deception he was perpetrating. The intention was to convince her that she was heading towards the third floor office as she had done every day since entering his employment."

The lift stopped at the third floor. Holmes pulled the large iron gate aside and beckoned for us to step out of the lift. We were faced with a solid looking oak door and along a long wall to the left of this was arranged a curious mixture of pots and stands of varying heights. A profusion of plant life filled the space and of those I recognised I could make out Kentia Palms and Sword Ferns and at least one large Yucca.

"A pretty display, eh, Inspector?"

Lestrade smiled weakly. "Yes, Mr Holmes. An odd assortment if you ask me. And exactly the same display on each of the first four upper floors."

"Patently. And on my earlier tour with the concierge, I was told that Mr Cartwright had paid a handsome sum for a local horticulturist to come in and assemble the collections only a week ago. Just before Miss Trelawney started work in fact."

"And is there any significance in that, Holmes?" I asked, unsure where he was heading with his observations.

"Yes. This was a key part of Mr Cartwright's diabolical scheme. Let us head up to the fourth floor and you will see why this was important."

Some minutes later we re-emerged from the lift to face an almost identical scene to that we had enjoyed on the third floor. Holmes headed towards the door of the office and turned to face us. "You will note how similar the two floors are. I have no doubt that when Miss Trelawney approached this entrance yesterday, accompanied by her very chatty employer, she was convinced that she was on the third floor."

We followed him into the outer room of the office. It was sparsely but expensively furnished and my eye was drawn immediately to a large panelled door on the far wall. Holmes followed my gaze.

"Yes, Watson – that is the door through to the room which Mr Cartwright occupied for most of yesterday morning. Had it been his regular room on the third floor, he would have had no means of reaching the stairwell or lift without being observed by his secretary. The only exit from that office is through the door in the outer room. But here on the fourth floor, he could take advantage of the one architectural feature that distinguishes this office from those on the lower floors."

At last, I understood what Holmes was alluding to. The four of us filed in to the back room where we could see to our left another panelled door – one that provided an alternative exit to the lift and stairwell.

"Very ingenious, Mr Holmes!" cried Lestrade, pointing to the door. "So that is how chummy here managed to reach the stairwell without being seen. It was then a simple matter of making his way down the stairs for the encounter with Edward Flanagan."

"That is correct. Violet Trelawney was unaware of the door because she was convinced that they were on the third floor. The careful positioning of the plants and stands outside the office has disguised the second exit - a task that was commissioned just before she began her new role."

"And yet, she knew instinctively that something was amiss," said I, unable to curb my excitement. "Holmes, you may remember that she confessed to feeling somewhat giddy while she sat in the room and imagined that the walls were closing in on her. It was less than twenty years ago that a medical colleague of mine, Dr Benjamin Ball, first coined the term *claustrophobia* which is now used to describe this feeling of anxiety. But in Miss Trelawney's case there was a particular reason for her discomfort. With the additional space taken up by the hidden corridor, the room in which she found herself was genuinely smaller than that on the third floor."

"Quite so!" agreed my colleague.

Inspector Lestrade moved a little closer towards Cartwright, who was looking considerably less composed than he had earlier. "But what about the gun and the coat and hat?" he queried.

"Where he left them yesterday, Inspector. I apologise for having badgered you earlier, about which areas of the building you had searched, but was fairly certain that our killer could not have disposed of the weapon or his disguise before your arrival yesterday. I took the liberty on my previous tour, but if you care to take a look in the large desk drawer to your left, you will see all of the offending items, including the revolver, tucked away at the bottom."

Lestrade stepped across to the desk. His face lit up as he opened the drawer and saw the evidence. "Well I never!" he uttered, retaining a keen eye on the increasingly fretful Cartwright. "I did think it was odd that our friend here should have made so much fuss about hearing the shot and insisting that he and Miss Trelawney trek down to the ground floor to speak to the concierge - especially when the young lady herself was minded to ignore it."

"Yes," agreed Holmes, "all part of his plan to create the illusion that he had been working in the back room all morning. Having shot Flanagan, I imagine it took him a few minutes to run up the three flights of stairs to the fourth floor, remove his disguise and hide both it and the revolver in the drawer. What was most telling was that he should be so keen to pick up Miss Trelawney's work tray in leaving the office. He believed he was removing the last trace of their presence in the fourth floor office. But, of course, he was wrong."

"I'm not sure I follow," said Lestrade.

I could not resist stealing Holmes' thunder. "Why, the curious matter of the missing Pearmain, of course." I looked across at Cartwright. "You didn't know anything about the apple she had hidden in the desk drawer, did you?"

Cartwright scowled and then raised his head in defiance. "No, damn you! I did not."

"And I think you'll find it's still in the drawer," Holmes mused. "A small detail, but a significant piece of evidence which will help to seal Mr Cartwright's fate. As for his motives, Lestrade, you might like to look into his business dealings in recent months. I understand he is close to bankruptcy having lost a small fortune investing in a property venture in Canada which has collapsed as a result of the recent Newfoundland Bank Crash. The last thing he wanted was a tenant who refused to pay the extortionate level of rent he demanded and one who seemed determined to upset the other occupants of the *white elephant* that is Ravensmere Towers."

Holmes' barbed comment prompted an angry snort from Cartwright, who stepped forward clenching his fists. Lestrade barred his way and stood eyeball to eyeball with the property owner until Cartwright stepped back, realising he had been outwitted. The inspector then produced a sturdy pair of handcuffs and secured his wrists.

On our way out of the office Holmes stopped to open the drawer of what had been Violet Trelawney's desk the previous day. As he had predicted, the apple lay where she had placed it.

Inspector Lestrade was ecstatic when we reached the lobby of the ground floor. He pushed Cartwright towards PC Clarke, who took charge of the dejected prisoner. James Mount looked on with evident discomfort, unsure whether he should be assisting the police officer and clearly troubled to see his employer in handcuffs.

Lestrade turned to the two of us as we trailed behind. "Mr Holmes, Dr Watson. I cannot thank you enough. I will, of course, mention your invaluable assistance when I speak again to the press."

Holmes responded in a hushed tone. "My dear Lestrade. I would much prefer it if you kept my name out of the papers on this occasion. The intelligence about Mr Cartwright's business affairs is not common knowledge and I would not like to have to reveal my source. I think it would be better for all concerned if you were to take full credit for the investigation."

The inspector could not have been happier. He accompanied us to the entrance and opened one of the large front doors before bidding us farewell. We stepped outside into the biting chill and thick acrid smog of the London air. Holmes took the lead, striding off towards Hyde Park, his eyes and ears alert to any sound of a nearby carriage. I pulled my coat collar up around my neck and shivered as I walked briskly to keep up with him.

************************

We were seated in front of a roaring coal fire back at Baker Street, cheered further by a glass of hot toddy and a stacked plate of sliced beef sandwiches, when at last I turned to Holmes and put to him the question I had wanted to ask a good half an hour before.

"So, was it the Danish King who told you about Archibald Cartwright's business affairs?"

Holmes rolled his whisky glass between his palms and looked across at me with a sly grin. "I did not think for a moment that you would leave the matter to rest, Watson. And the straight answer to your question is 'Yes'. The king is clearly a man who likes to keep abreast of current affairs, both at home and abroad. In a quiet moment, he asked me what cases I was working on. Without giving it much thought, I mentioned that I was assisting Scotland Yard on a murder case in one of London's most prestigious new office buildings. 'That must be the strange occurrence at Ravensmere Towers,' he said, before going on to say that he had read the piece in the *Daily Telegraph*.

"I could not deny that they were one and the same, to which the king added: 'You may not be aware of this, Mr Holmes, but my son knows Archibald Cartwright, the owner of the building. In fact, the two of them were at Eton together and it was he who first encouraged Valdemar to begin investing in some of these perilous financial schemes in Canada. Cartwright has recently been ruined by his own property investments in Newfoundland. Clearly, I do not know the circumstances surrounding the death, but would not be at all surprised if the man had a hand in it.' It seems he was not wrong, Watson."

"No, and a very timely and useful piece of information, I'd say. That ceremonial luncheon wasn't such a waste of your time, after all," I quipped.

He looked up to the small presentation box on the mantelpiece and grinned again. "As ever, you are right, my friend."

# 3. A Study in Verse

While Sherlock Holmes was a prodigious reader of books on a wide variety of subjects, it would be fair to say that he was rarely interested in anything of a fictional or romantic nature. While professionally he revelled in the unusual, the unknown and the generally inexplicable, his taste in literature was categorically prosaic. It therefore came as something of a surprise to find him reading a book of poetry when I called in to Baker Street one afternoon in the September of 1895.

"Now, there is a sight I have rarely witnessed," said I, entering the upstairs room and noting the small volume of *Japanese Style Short-Form Poetry* he held in his long thin fingers. I was tickled at the notion that Holmes should be reading something so avant-garde. I took a chair close to the fireplace and waited for an explanation.

"Watson! A pleasure to see you on this bright, autumnal day. Your eyes have not deceived you, my friend. I am indeed reading, and enjoying, this fine collection of verse. Ordinarily, I cannot see any virtue in the rambling and meandering lines which pass for poetry in our literary culture. Our best known writers seem to take great delight in saying in a few hundred disorderly words what a dictionary compiler might neatly summarise in a dozen. I read to get the nub of an issue, to be told all that I need to know in as few words as possible. Poetry is anathema to my ordered and focused mind."

"Come then - what is this collection you seem so thoroughly engrossed in? I have never heard of *Japanese style short-form poetry.*"

"We have much to learn about ancient Japanese culture, my friend. And the Asian approach to poetry has much to commend it. For centuries, the Japanese have perfected the art of stand-alone *hokku* verse, which sometimes serves as a prequel to a much longer composition. More recently, some writers have begun to adapt hokku poetry into a more concentrated, shorter form of poetry, which may typically juxtapose two distinct refrains, usually on a theme of nature. Masaoka Shiki, a young writer in his twenties, uses the term *haiku* to describe this new approach."

I was still not sure I fully understood what was so different about this haiku poetry, so asked him to elaborate further.

"I first came across the literary form while reading Hendrik Doeff's *Recollections of Japan*. You may remember that he was a former Commissioner for the Dejima trading post in Nagasaki, which the Dutch East India Company held on to in the early part of this century despite our British claims to the territory. Doeff was the author of a Dutch-Japanese dictionary and was the first westerner to pen some of this short-form poetry.

"A haiku poem strips away all but the bare essentials of the verse and follows a rigid, highly-structured, layout. Perhaps the best known form is a verse of three lines which contains exactly seventeen syllables. The first and last lines have five syllables apiece, while the middle line contains no more and no less than seven. The art is in presenting a poem which conforms precisely to the accepted arrangement, with no superfluous words or syllables. Short, specific and to the point, a form of poetry I can appreciate."

"And is this a collection written by Mr Doeff?" I asked.

"No, his early attempts were, at best, experimental. The adoption of haiku poetry in Europe has moved the art on significantly beyond his stanzas. What I am particularly interested in, within this slim volume, is a section on crime-related haiku, written by a young poet called Edwin Halvergate. He manages to describe a fictional murder and within the same verse provides clues to the identity of the killer. Let me give you an example."

Holmes then read aloud:

"Man shot for money.
Robber – Daniel, Tim or Kyle?
Killer in denial."

I looked at him bemused. "Well, it is certainly a short poem Holmes! Let me look at it on the page."

He got up from his seat and came across to me with the book, holding it up and pointing to the relevant verse. I read it to myself and then said: "So, the man is killed during a robbery and we have three suspects, each of which claims to be innocent of the crime. The poem then invites us to guess who the killer is."

Holmes chuckled. "That's it, Watson. You have it. See how the short-form does not obscure the key facts. But the verse is not inviting you to guess who committed the crime - it tells you. Look at the last line: 'killer in denial'. Yes, it's telling us that the suspect denies murder, but 'denial' is also an anagram of *Daniel*. He is the guilty man."

"Very clever, Holmes," I mused. "Let me have another, now that I've got the gist."

Holmes flicked on a couple of pages and picked out another poem:

"Jane dead – knew killer.

Initial clues point to him.
Mark, Kane, Fred or Jim?"

This time I worked through the logic of the key facts. "We have another murder. This time, of a lady called Jane, who evidently knew the person who killed her. The poem again gives us a number of suspects, based on some early clues. But I'm guessing in this case that 'initial clues' has a double meaning. If we look at the initial letters which begin each line, they spell out the name of our murderer – JIM. How's that, Holmes?"

"Perfect! Of course, these are but introductory examples of Halvergate's craft. His haiku get more intricate and complex as one progresses through the book. But then I would expect no less, given that Edwin Halvergate is not only a talented poet, but also a gifted logician who once studied under Professor Moriarty."

I recoiled at the name. "Then your poetry reading is not for idle pleasure. Has this Edwin Halvergate followed Moriarty into a life of criminality?"

Holmes returned to his chair, closed the book and placed it on a pile of other manuscripts and papers to his left. "I am afraid so. He is fast becoming a major player in the criminal underworld of the capital. I have heard it said that he is trying to emulate his one-time academic mentor and resurrect the evil empire that Moriarty once led. It is my personal mission to prevent that from happening."

"Agreed, but how will you work against him? I imagine that Halvergate - like Moriarty before him - is rarely at the scene of a crime or directly involved in any of the nefarious activities he commissions."

Holmes nodded. "That is correct. But like his predecessor, it will be his *hubris*, his fatal pride, which will bring his downfall. Halvergate is clever, and certainly ambitious, but he is no Moriarty. He is constantly risking exposure and relying on criminal associates who show him no loyalty. And he has not been Machiavellian enough to rule as the Professor did. It will only be a matter of time before he slips again, and when he does, I shall be waiting."

With that, Holmes refused to elaborate any further on the exploits of Edwin Halvergate. We moved on to talk about the audacious crime that had taken place two days before, which was still dominating the headlines of most provincial newspapers. Namely, the theft of the Football Association Challenge Cup – an expensive silver trophy which had been taken from a shop window display in Birmingham and, for which, the police had offered a £10 reward. Holmes told me in confidence that he had already offered his services in the pursuit of the thief or thieves, and had yet to hear from the Birmingham City Police who had, thus far, chosen to pursue the case on their own.

*************************

It was in early December of that same year that Edwin Halvergate was to occupy Holmes' thoughts once more. And, ironically, it was the still missing FA Cup that was to have a bearing on the events that followed.

I had just returned home one Friday from a visit to an elderly patient in Kensington whose neuralgia I had been treating for the previous six months. As I put my key into the lock of the door, I was greeted by a short telegram boy who had just arrived by bicycle. Having established that I was the intended recipient, he thrust a telegram into my hand and asked me to sign his log book to confirm that the message had been delivered. When I had stepped inside and relieved myself of my heavy medical bag, I opened the telegram. It read: *'Impending visit from Birmingham Police...come to BS immediately = SH.'*

I smirked at Holmes' brevity. In his customary manner, he had shown little regard for the fact that I had a business to run and patients to attend. Fortuitously, I had no other calls of an urgent nature, so acceded to his request that afternoon and hailed a cab a short while later. When I reached Baker Street, Mrs Hudson greeted me warmly and relieved me of my coat, hat and scarf before whispering that an 'Inspector Walcott' had arrived not twenty minutes earlier and was already seated with Holmes. I smiled and nodded my thanks.

When I entered the study, Inspector Walcott rose from his seat and extended me a very cordial welcome. He was a thickset man in his late-forties, with thinning hair and bushy grey whiskers and sideburns, and wore a loose-fitting tweed suit with brown ankle boots. His cheeks were flushed, but his eyes bright and alert. A broad smile was etched across his craggy features and a large, bulbous nose hinted at his inclination towards strong liquor. I could see that Holmes had already drawn the same conclusion, for a large whisky glass sat on the small chestnut table to our guest's side. Holmes, I noted, had not joined him in partaking of the single malt.

Walcott's accent was as distinct as it was deep. There was no mistaking his Black Country inflection, but the intonation was but a low growl, accentuated by a wheezy breathlessness which forced him to clear his throat or cough every three or four sentences. He was clearly not a man in the best of health, but seemed unconcerned and certainly jovial enough.

With the introductions concluded, Holmes offered to provide me with a short précis of the reason for Walcott's visit: "Watson, the good inspector has brought us some interesting news. You will recall our earlier deliberations over the criminal aspirations of a certain Edwin Halvergate, the would-be gang master and one-time poet?"

"Yes, indeed," I replied, noting that Walcott had raised an eyebrow at the mention of Halvergate's poetic inclinations.

"Well, I have reason to believe that Halvergate has been trying to extend his influence beyond the capital and into the heart of the country's second city. Inspector Walcott is the officer in charge of the investigations into the disappearance of the FA Cup. His contacts in the Birmingham underworld have suggested that the crime was perpetrated by a criminal gang from the Seven Dials area of London. They apparently planned the robbery to prove a point - that they are capable of carrying out a daring theft, in the full glare of publicity, and in an area outside of their usual domain. I have been telling the inspector all about Halvergate's felonious proclivities. That he lives in a very considerable town house in the heart of the Seven Dials, close to Convent Garden, cannot be a coincidence."

On hearing this, I could not disguise my general annoyance at the extraordinary efforts that appeared to be in hand to locate a single sports trophy and Holmes' insistence that I drop everything and race across to Baker Street. Granted, the FA Cup was a hugely symbolic piece of silverware to football fanatics across the country, but did it really warrant the attention of the world's first consulting detective? My irritation must have shown, for Walcott clearly felt he had interject, to explain the more significant part of the story, which involved a crime more serious than the initial robbery.

"Doctor Watson, I apologise, for you did not get to hear my full account of what we have been faced with in conducting our enquiries around the missing trophy," said Walcott, reaching for a grubby handkerchief, into which he coughed a couple of times. "If Mr Holmes will forgive the interruption, I will acquaint you with the basic facts."

A frown flashed briefly across Holmes' face, before he smiled and then nodded for Walcott to continue.

"At first, we imagined this was an opportunist robbery carried out by some near-do-well with an eye for the scrap value of the silver. And yet, none of the local characters who might ordinarily be in the market for disposing of such an item knew anything about the theft. It was only when we did the rounds of our small band of informants – mainly the cabbies and ladies of the night that operate around the Bull Ring - and offered up the inducement of a few free shillings, that tongues began to wag. While no one knew their names, it seemed to be common knowledge that two Londoners had appeared in the city, visiting local silversmiths and asking about who might be in possession of the FA Cup. The day after the robbery, the two men had checked out of their expensive hotel rooms and caught a cab to Birmingham New Street. The cabbie that had driven them to the railway station heard them talking about 'getting back to business in the Seven Dials.'"

After clearing his throat and taking a couple of large gulps from the whisky glass, Walcott resumed his narrative. "On visiting the hotel concerned, we learned that the pair had used false names in checking in to their rooms and coming and going for the four nights of their stay. But it appears that their arrival in the city had not gone unnoticed by our large fraternity of Irish felons. What the men didn't know was that their movements, in staking out the Newton Row shop of Mr William Shillcock in Aston, where the trophy was on temporary display, were being shadowed by the Delaney Gang from the Snow Hill district of Birmingham.

"The Delaneys are best known for their coining operations and strong arm tactics in keeping rival gangs out of the city. They appear to have taken umbrage that the Londoners should encroach on their turf and attempt to steal the trophy. But they acted cleverly in responding to the challenge. The word of one or two of our other informants is that they allowed the theft to take place, and then intercepted the two after the robbery and quietly, but firmly, relieved them of the stolen trophy. Outnumbered and outgunned, there was little the pair could do but return to their hotel and then travel back to London the following day – no doubt with their tails between their legs."

"And what of the trophy now?" I asked; keen to know if Walcott had recovered the stolen item, given that he seemed to know so much about what had occurred.

"No luck there, I'm afraid, Doctor. My hunch is that the Delaney Gang have already melted it down and knocked out a hundred or more counterfeit half-crowns. I'm not so much bothered about that given recent events. You see, four nights ago a more serious crime was committed and it seems the Delaneys had a hand in it." A further cough followed, after which Walcott drained the last of his whisky. Holmes rose quietly and refilled the glass as our guest then carried on.

"For seven years, we have had a Detective Sergeant by the name of Clive Delamare working for the Birmingham City force. A quiet man in his late-fifties, whom I always saw as a capable and trustworthy officer. I now have reason to believe that his real name was, in fact, *Clive Delaney* and in serving with the City Police he has operated very cleverly to prevent us from dealing effectively with the threats posed by the criminal gang to which he was related. The gang has always managed to stay one step ahead of us, whenever we attempted to investigate their activities or disrupt their counterfeiting operations. Clive Delaney was one of their own and while he has proved to be a diligent officer in bringing to book scores of felons from the city's underworld, he has acted to shield his family from the official exposure they deserve. And yet, on Monday evening, he appears to have been shot by his own gang members in a flagrant and bloody murder on one of Birmingham's main thoroughfares."

I was intrigued to hear this. "And do you know how and why he was killed, Inspector?" I enquired.

"Well, that's where it begins to get more complicated. Sergeant Delamare, as we knew him, had just finished a long shift a few minutes after ten o'clock that evening. As he stepped outside the main door of the Steelhouse Lane police station, he was approached by three men in long, dark frock coats, one of whom drew a revolver and pointed it directly at him. We have three witnesses to what then occurred. There was some arguing between the gunman and Delamare, although all of the men were clearly trying to keep their voices down and avoid attracting attention. The witnesses said that Delamare was doing most of the remonstrating and did not look to be intimidated by the men. During the exchange, one man was heard to say 'It's a question of family honour', to which Delamare replied 'Go to Hell! I'm your father – don't you dare talk to me about honour!'"

"So, a distinct family connection with the gang!" observed my colleague.

"Certainly, Mr Holmes," wheezed Walcott, pausing for a couple of seconds. "Immediately after that, there was a loud bang – the result of a single shot from the revolver – and Sergeant Delamare collapsed onto the cobbles, having been fatally shot through the chest. The three men then ran off, dodging into a passageway off Steelhouse Lane. Rather fortuitously for us, they could not have picked a worse escape route. It was a narrow lane, at the top end of which were stationed two uniformed constables who had just heard the shot. They tackled the men they came face to face with and during the struggle managed to floor two of them, who were then arrested. One was found to be carrying a revolver. The third man, who had remained at the edge of the affray, managed to escape and is still at large."

"Were the officers able to get a good look at the third man?" Holmes enquired keenly.

"No. And the two men we arrested have steadfastly refused to say anything about him." He passed Holmes some photographs of the men in custody. "I thought you might like these. Frank Delaney is the taller of the two, with the distinct jet-black hair."

This time it was I who quizzed the inspector. "You hinted earlier that there were some complications. So far, it all seems fairly straightforward to me. Sergeant Delamare has been living a double life and is a father to one of the gang. Clearly he has done something in his role as a police officer which has undermined or threatened his family in some way, and the son has attempted to warn him off. Faced with the uncompromising attitude of his father, he has then shot the officer in a fit of rage."

"Bravo, Watson! A very plausible explanation. And one that I am sure is very close to the truth. But the complication to which the inspector refers is not around *why* the crime was commissioned."

"That is correct," chimed Walcott. "One of the men in custody is Thomas Logan, a heavy for the gang, who has made certain distinct noises, no doubt seeking some leniency for himself. He has hinted that Delamare was about to tip us off about the theft of the stolen trophy, as the operation to dispossess the

London men of the booty had not been officially authorised by the hierarchy of the Delaney Gang. It seems that the three men were tasked with warning Delamare, but exceeded their brief. Logan has made it plain that he had nothing to do with the shooting and the murder weapon looks to be the gun that his colleague was arrested with."

"And who is the other man in custody?" I asked.

"His name is Frank Delaney, and Logan has confirmed that he is indeed Clive Delamare's son. The twenty-nine year old was previously unknown to us. He has said only that he arrived in this country from Ireland a month ago. He also said that the gun is his and Logan did not fire it. Until yesterday, I believed we had a rock solid case against the man. Each witness picked him out of the identity parade we held at the Steelhouse Lane station. And all three were certain that he was the man they saw holding and firing the gun."

"So, how can you possibly doubt that Frank Delaney is the culprit?" I countered, astounded that there could be any degree of uncertainty.

"Well, two things, Doctor; Firstly, the fingerprints on the revolver. I know the science is still rudimentary, but the prints we observed on the handle and trigger of the weapon do not match those of the suspect. His prints are on the gun, but only along the barrel, which suggests that one of the others passed the gun to him and he held it that way before placing it inside his frock coat, where we later recovered it. The other reason I now entertain some doubts, is because of the arrival of this." He held within his coarse, plump fingers a small white envelope.

"The letter arrived by post yesterday, addressed to me. I was about to pass it to Mr Holmes when you arrived, Dr Watson. I will do so now, and the two of you can make of it what you will. Certainly it is a very ambiguous note, but does make me wonder if we have arrested the right man."

The letter was handed across to Holmes, who immediately took up his magnifying glass and began to inspect both the envelope and its contents in his usual meticulous fashion. He examined every inch of the document, holding it up to the light at one point and smelling the paper for any trace of evidence that might be discernible. Inspector Walcott looked on incredulously.

When at last Holmes had completed his scrutiny, he passed across to me the typewritten note and its envelope. It read as follows:

*My dearest Inspector Walcott,*

*No doubt you are well immersed in your investigations into the disappearance of the FA Challenge Cup. The case has attracted lots of press attention, so I am used to seeing your face in the newspapers. The fact that you haven't found it is testimony indeed to the efficiency of the counterfeiting empire which a certain criminal family seem to operate with relative impunity in your expanding city. I know this because some of those close to me had a hand in taking the trophy and were duped by the Delaneys, an act that will have continuing repercussions.*

*Detective Sergeant Clive Delamare had for some time been a close ally of mine and I was happy to pay him handsomely for the titbits of information he was able to pass to me about particular felons or police officers that I might have an interest in, as my associates have begun to extend their operations outside of the capital. However, the one crucial fact he chose not to share with me was his familial connection to the Delaneys – something, I imagine, you were also unaware of.*

73

*In the summer of last year, I discussed with him our plan to steal the football trophy as a gesture to the Birmingham underworld. He realised of course that the robbery would jeopardise the Delaney position. So he took it upon himself to tell his oldest son what we had in mind, imagining that his offspring might then take steps to ensure that the family were seen to be above suspicion and completely blameless of any involvement in the theft. But his son is a chancer, without his father's caution and guile. He saw an opportunity to outfox my colleagues. He underestimated me and the lengths I will now go to, to get even with his kind.*

*When my associates returned to London, I knew that Clive Delamare had betrayed me. I made contact with him and told him what was to be done. He was to broker a deal with the Delaneys whereby the trophy would be returned to me and the family would, from that point on, operate under my control. Any divergence from this would result in the wholesale assassination of their leaders. It was then that he confessed to being Clive Delaney, one of three men who effectively controlled the Delaney Gang. He explained that his son had acted without authorisation and would be punished for what he had done. He went on to say that he was in no position to broker the deal I had insisted upon as the family would never agree to it. I am not an unreasonable man, Inspector Walcott. I said that I understood his difficulties and proffered a final solution – to surrender the trophy, kill his son and return to Ireland. It seems that he has been unsuccessful in adhering to my request and his son has, yet again, taken matters into his own hands.*

*At this point, you may be wondering why I should insist on telling you any of this. Well, it is just that I believe we can help each other. You see, the son has not only refused to bend to my will, but has also now instigated his own coup d'état and seized control of all the family's affairs. As such, he is my chief rival in the midlands and I want him removed from that position. Something you can do in securing his conviction for murder.*

*You still have some work to do, however, and I suggest you invite Mr Sherlock Holmes – another of my adversaries, but a much more likeable one – to assist you in carrying out your task. Call it honour among thieves, or some sort of felonious chivalric code, but I will not let it be said that it was me that told you specifically who killed Clive Delaney. That said, you can take the following facts as gospel:*

1. *Clive Delaney, better known as Sergeant Delamare, was the intended target – unbeknown to his two accomplices, the guilty man fully intended to kill him.*

2. *The dead man was shot by his own biological son – he had no other children older or younger than twenty-nine years of age.*

3. *Any eye witnesses you have to the killing can be relied upon – they will have witnessed the death of your sergeant at the hands of his son.*

4. *The gun used in the attack belonged to Frank Delaney.*

5. *But the killer was not Frank Delaney.*

*I trust that this information will speed your endeavours.*

*Yours very sincerely,*

*A concerned citizen*

I looked up in astonishment when I had finished reading the note. "But this is nonsensical, Holmes. Everything points to Frank Delaney, and yet we are to believe that he is not the killer. If this is written by Edwin Halvergate, it is another of his riddles, further evidence of his flowery poetic notions. He is seeking to make fools of us all."

"My thoughts exactly," added Walcott.

"Nonsense! It all seems perfectly clear to me. The answer lies not just in what is written, but what is not written - like those earlier haiku poems, we have to be mindful of inference. And I have a firm plan to finally expose the killer, which will require us to catch a train this very evening." Holmes glanced at his pocket watch and jumped up with enthusiasm. "We have sufficient time to pack a few essentials and to pick up anything you require from your home on the way, Watson, before catching the 6.30 from Euston to Birmingham New Street. We will rely on Inspector Walcott to recommend a suitable hotel close to the station for our short overnight stay."

My attempt to voice some opposition to the plan was soon drowned out by the noise of Holmes shouting down the stairs with various requests of Mrs Hudson. Ten minutes later, the three of us were seated in a cab heading towards my home, for a short stop on the way to Euston. I took the opportunity to quiz Holmes once more about the letter.

"How can you be certain the note was written by Edwin Halvergate?"

"Why, who else would be in a position to do so and who else would mention me specifically as an *adversary*?" he retorted. "You know my methods, Watson. I have made it my business to know the minutiae of Edwin Halvergate's life. The tell-tale signs were there. The Seven Dials postmark on the envelope, the stationery purchased from Henry Stone & Son Ltd, the distinctive printing of the Merritt typewriter and the faint whiff of camphor from the hair oil he uses with some vanity to counter his accelerated hair loss."

"Remarkable, Mr Holmes!" spluttered Inspector Walcott, in awe of my friend's revelations. I had to admit that his case was pretty persuasive. While it may not have stood up in a court of law, it was enough to convince me that Halvergate was indeed the architect of this curious chain of events.

We arrived at Euston with about eight minutes to spare, sufficient time for us to secure a first-class compartment on the train and to avail ourselves of copies of the half-penny *Evening News*. When seated in the carriage, Holmes let out a big sigh and pointed to a headline at the bottom of the front page, which read: '*Two bodies recovered from Thames – murder feared*'.

"It seems that Edwin Halvergate has finally taken steps to assert his authority over his criminal associates. He has no doubt completed his reading of Niccolò Machiavelli's *The Prince* and now believes that the way to maintain the discipline of his henchmen is to operate with ruthless expediency, the ends justifying whatever means he chooses. The bodies recovered from the river are of two well-dressed men in their early-thirties, whose wallets had not been taken. Each had been garrotted and both had distinctive wasp tattoos on their forearms – the symbol under which the gang operates. I think we can safely say that they were the hapless London thieves of the FA Cup and this is firm evidence that Halvergate is serious about his threat to assassinate key members of the Delaney family. I fear you may have some serious gang violence to contend with in the coming months, Inspector Walcott."

The inspector nodded, but remained silent, taking time to read the full details of the story in his copy of the newspaper. Some minutes later, Holmes sought to raise Walcott's spirits with a plan to reveal who had killed Sergeant Clive Delamare. On reaching Birmingham, the police officer was to make his way to the Steelhouse Lane police station and have Frank Delaney moved with some uproar from his holding cell to an area of solitary confinement, where he would be detained overnight in strict secrecy. At eleven o'clock, Walcott was to inform Thomas Logan that his colleague had managed to escape from Steelhouse Lane and was now on the run. Furthermore, Logan was to be told that he was free to leave the police station, as the detectives had concluded that there was little evidence for his culpability in the murder.

Trusting in Holmes, the inspector readily agreed to the plan. He was then asked to meet us at eleven-thirty in the foyer of the *Grand Hotel*, which he had earlier recommended for our stay in the city.

When we reached Birmingham New Street it was a little after ten-fifteen. We departed from the train and said our farewells to Walcott, making our way to the hotel with the directions he had given us. The *Grand Hotel* on Colmore Row was a spectacular seven-storey building constructed in a French Renaissance style. Our individual bedrooms were palatial by London standards and the hotel was furnished with a dining room, crush room and drawing room of the most flamboyant designs. Holmes insisted on booking the two rooms for our stay while I remained seated in the extensive lobby. When he returned from the reception desk, he handed me a key for 'Room 238' and announced that he had some business to attend to before our planned meeting with Inspector Walcott and needed some time alone. I watched him head off towards the main stairwell and decided to undertake a short tour of the hotel as I awaited his return.

Shortly before eleven-thirty, I made my way back down to the foyer. Inspector Walcott had just arrived, and sat on the plush seating looking distinctly drained and breathless. He explained that it had been a long day, but seemed pleased that Holmes' strategy had been carried out as planned. Frank Delaney had been placed in a solitary cell, with only Walcott and a duty sergeant knowing of his whereabouts. And Thomas Logan had been released, scurrying away from the police station, barely able to believe his luck.

The two of us chatted for the next twenty minutes while we waited for Holmes to join us. The hotel seemed quiet that evening, with just a few guests returning from their evening excursions to the theatres, restaurants and music halls of the city. At one point I saw a particularly well turned out couple in full evening dress arrive by carriage. As the hotel doorman greeted them, I watched as a dark faced, shabbily-attired workman in a cloth cap attempted to sneak in before the couple, cheekily tipping his cap as he did so. He had clearly underestimated the adroitness of the doorman, however, who seized the back of his collar and pulled him to one side, while allowing the well-dressed night-goers to enter the hotel.

Inspector Walcott had also witnessed the fracas and as I jumped up, he struggled to raise himself from his comfortable seat in order to assist the doorman who was still arguing with the ragamuffin. As we approached, the captive let out an unrestrained guffaw, and then said, in a very familiar voice: "Inspector Walcott, Dr Watson, I would be grateful if you could please ask our friend here to release his iron-like grip from my delicate collar. The man is half throttling me!"

"Holmes!?" My exclamation was sufficient for the doorman to release his prisoner.

"I am so sorry, sir! I had no idea you knew these gentlemen," stuttered the red-faced doorman looking across at Walcott, who already had his police badge out on display. The doorman then glanced back at Holmes, expecting some sort of explanation.

Holmes reached for a pocket and placed a half-crown in the man's hand, while offering a short apology. "My good man, it is reassuring to know that the *Grand Hotel* employs such dedicated and resourceful men. In a short while we are likely to have need of your considerable talents. Within ten minutes, two well-dressed men in their late-twenties will attempt to enter this foyer. Please do not bar their entrance. Say only that 'Frank' has tipped you off about their arrival and they are to make their way to Room 238. Is that understood?"

The bewildered doorman looked once more to Walcott, who merely added, "Rest assured, this is police business. I will provide you with a full explanation in due course. For the moment, I would be grateful if you would go along with Mr Holmes' request." The doorman nodded his consent and the three of us headed off in the direction of the main stairwell.

A few minutes later, we were seated comfortably in the confines of my bedroom. Holmes had returned briefly to his own room to pick up a change of clothing and was now in the process of shedding his working man's attire and removing some of the theatrical grease paint he had applied earlier to complete his disguise. In the warm glow of the gas lamps, he was explaining with some haste what he had been up to.

"Watson, it would be as well if you were to have your old service revolver to hand in readiness for our visitors. I am glad now that I reminded you to pack it earlier this evening. We can take no chances with the Delaneys – they are formidable folk. My disguise was necessary to allow me to follow Thomas Logan when he was released from the police station at eleven o'clock. I pursued him for a short distance until he hailed a cab. I heard him ask for the *Anchor Inn* on Tenant Street. When he was safely on his way, I took another cab and followed him to the public house, which I entered shortly afterwards. The crowd assembled there took little interest in me such was the furore that had greeted the arrival of Logan. It was not difficult for me to spot the Delaney leader, who was now patting Logan on the back and calling for drinks all round.

"Seizing the initiative, I approached the man and announced discreetly that I was the cabbie who had assisted Frank Delaney in his escape from Steelhouse Lane. He stepped away from the others and pulled me towards him. I explained that time was of the essence, as Frank had asked for immediate assistance – he was hiding out in Room 238 of the *Grand Hotel* and required some help in escaping from the city. Continuing with the charade, I then added that Frank was keen to avoid any unwanted attention and had suggested that if two well-dressed members of the gang could meet him in his hotel room at midnight armed with a gun it would allow him to make good his escape. The circumstances, the opportunism and the directness of the approach seemed to work in my favour. Not for a moment did he seem to doubt my story and I was able to slip away from the inn minutes later, a few counterfeit coins the richer. And now, I fear, we have but a short while before we receive a telling knock on the door."

My colleague was not wrong. He had barely enough time to pull on a short black jacket and grab the small cudgel he had brought with him, when there was a loud rap on the bedroom door. Holmes raised an upright forefinger to his lips in order that we remain silent and stepped deftly towards the door. He opened it swiftly and stood behind the door as two burly characters entered the room at speed, the man at the front wielding a revolver. As both men turned to their left and saw Inspector Walcott and I the weapon was raised in our direction. I was too slow in bringing my own revolver to a firing position and feared we were done for. At the same time,

Holmes stepped out from behind the door and brought his weighty cudgel down on the wrist of the intruder. The man's arm fell away towards the floor and the revolver slipped from his hand. He cried out in pain and his colleague scrambled forward, trying to make a grab for the gun. But Inspector Walcott was already well ahead of him and kicked the weapon away from his grasp before flooring the man with a strong punch to the head. I had my own revolver pointing at both men before Holmes then spoke.

"Gentlemen, how good of you to put in an appearance! I am reassured that my cameo as a Birmingham cab driver was sufficiently convincing to lure you here. And it seems as if my little ruse has drawn the principal players to perform for us. Inspector Walcott, you are already acquainted with Thomas Logan, but you can now meet the murderer of Sergeant Delamare."

With a look of some concern, Walcott stared at the tall man with the distinctive crop of jet-black hair who towered above the broad-shouldered Logan. "But how is this possible, Mr Holmes? I left Frank Delaney under lock and key only a short time ago. He could not have escaped in that time, met with you earlier and then made his way here."

"Indeed, he could not. You see, this is not Frank, but his identical twin-brother, *Sean* Delaney. The same man who has now assumed control over the Delaney Gang and made such an enemy of Edwin Halvergate."

The mention of Halvergate's name brought a sharp response from the injured Sean Delaney. "He's the man you really ought to be locking up, Walcott. I don't know who these gentlemen are, but they seem to have outfoxed us this evening." He then looked directly at Holmes with an expression of pure hatred. "My friends will ensure that I escape the noose. Be certain of that. But as a gang we are finished. Halvergate has already begun to target my men and disrupt all of our operations. He even had my own father in his pocket."

Inspector Walcott was quick to defend his former colleague. "Your father had more sense than to challenge Halvergate and you placed him in an impossible position. He acted only to stop you being killed and you reacted by taking his life. Something you will have to live with, and explain to your younger twin-brother."

Delaney looked down and grimaced as he pulled his wrist to his chest. He had nothing further to say.

We accompanied the men down to the foyer and thanked the doorman for his earlier assistance. While Holmes and I kept guard over the pair, Inspector Walcott went off to despatch a telegram to the police station. Fifteen minutes later a squad of four uniformed constables arrived with handcuffs and led the gang members away.

Before his departure, Walcott could not resist asking Holmes a final question. "Mr Holmes, Dr Watson. I am forever indebted to both of you for your assistance today. That you have achieved so much in such a short space of time is truly beyond me. But I am intrigued to know how you could be so certain that Sean Delaney and, indeed, Thomas Logan, would come to the hotel room, rather than any other members of the gang."

Holmes eyes were wide with delight. "My dear Inspector. Sean Delaney has staged a recent takeover within the gang. He may have assumed control, but would not have trusted anyone other than those close to him. As the man in jeopardy was his own brother, it seemed fair to assume that he would wish to be involved, accompanied by the ever-present Logan.

Delaney is a man who leads from the front, something that has now signalled a death knell for the family in this city."

"So it would seem," I added, shaking Walcott warmly by the hand. We said our goodbyes and watched as the dogged, but weary, inspector left the hotel.

The next morning, Holmes and I were up bright and early to catch one of the first trains back to London. It was almost midday when we arrived back at Baker Street. Mrs Hudson greeted us at the door, looking relieved that we had returned in good health following our impromptu departure the evening before. A short while later we were sat comfortably in front of a crackling fire enjoying some tea and buttered crumpets.

When Mrs Hudson came to retrieve our plates and cups, she carried with her a small parcel. "I forgot to mention it earlier, Mr Holmes, but this arrived for you about ten o'clock this morning." She handed him the parcel and proceeded to clear away the crockery.

Instinctively, Holmes began to examine the packaging and even before he had unwrapped it announced, "Curious, Watson. This is from Edwin Halvergate. Let's see what it contains." He removed the brown paper covering to reveal a small book and flicked through the first few pages. "Mr Halvergate certainly loves his poetry. This is a second volume of haiku verse, this one written exclusively by our man. And how touching, he has dedicated it to me."

I could tell that Holmes' sarcasm masked a genuine concern. "What does it say?" I asked.

"A single line – 'Thank you for your recent help at the *Grand Hotel* – EH'. He is well informed, Watson. And no doubt it will not be the last time we hear from Edwin Halvergate."

With that he placed the book upon the mantelpiece and refused to discuss the matter further.

I left Holmes a short while later, picking up my overnight case from the hallway and saying goodbye to Mrs Hudson. The weather had taken a distinct turn and a dark, mackerel-coloured sky announced that heavy storm clouds were on their way. As I stood awaiting the arrival of a carriage, I glanced back at the upstairs window. And in that moment I realised, that however many criminals, swindlers, thieves and fraudsters we managed to outwit, there would always be another lurking in the shadows, waiting to strike. I shivered at the thought.

# 4. The Case of the Cuneiform Suicide Note

It was towards the end of July 1903 that I returned from a short break in Ireland; a trip occasioned by the death of a close medical colleague who had established a successful medical practice in Cork some ten years earlier. Relieved to be home, I paid the cab driver and dropped my heavy bags and cases in the hallway. A quick tour of the house suggested that everything was as I had left it, and satisfied that my sanctuary was still secure and free from leaks, wind damage and insect infestations, I took a seat in the front parlour to catch my breath. Scarcely had I time to sit back on the comfortable *bergère* when my repose was cut short by a loud and distinctive rap on the front door. It was clear that my colleague had timed his visit to perfection.

When I opened the door, Sherlock Holmes stood before me in a fashionable tweed suit and wide blue necktie. He gave me a broad grin and tipped the peak of his deerstalker with the top of a thin walking stick. "Welcome back, Watson. Or, should I say, 'a top o' the mornin' to ya'?"

"Holmes, you must be very well informed about my comings and goings, for I have only just this minute returned."

The smile did not diminish. "Truth be told, my friend, I had completely forgotten when you were due back and wrongly believed you had made the crossing from Ireland yesterday. You must therefore forgive the intrusion, but I just wanted to be sure that you were still free to come with me this evening to the Library of the British Museum."

Never one to hide an indiscretion, I felt it best to acknowledge that I had absolutely no recollection of any such appointment.

"Tut, tut, old man, it seems that I am not the only one prone to periodic memory loss," Holmes retorted. "A little over a month ago, I mentioned to you that Dr Henry Canham-Page, the celebrated archaeologist, was due to give a lecture on the subject of the *Cuneiform Records of Mesopotamia* and you readily agreed that we ought to attend. His talk is at seven o'clock this evening. If you do still wish to come along, I can call for you at six-thirty."

Feeling somewhat embarrassed at my *faux pas*, I acquiesced and said that I would be pleased to accompany him. With a distinct spring in his step, Holmes then turned and headed off with a cheery, "Farewell then, Doctor – until this evening."

When the hansom arrived at the agreed time I was hovering on the doorstep, loath to keep Holmes waiting and knowing full well how much he liked to get front row seats at any academic lecture so as not to be disturbed or distracted by others in the audience. After a brief ride, we pulled up to the venue in good time and with just a short queue outside were ushered into the British Museum Reading Room with ten minutes to spare.

The reading room provided the perfect setting for the lecture. Situated in the centre of the building, it had an impressive domed ceiling some 140 feet in diameter, modelled, we were told, on the great Pantheon of Rome. And all around us were book stacks, providing over twenty-four miles of shelving for the hundreds of thousands of books housed in the library. It was therefore with some anticipation that we settled down only a few feet from the small raised stage, blackboard and lectern and awaited the arrival of Dr Henry Canham-Page.

Amid the general chit chat of the expectant audience, I took the opportunity to ask Holmes a discreet question. "Holmes. I do not wish to sound ill-informed, but having had little time to think about the nature of the lecture this evening, I find myself in the unenviable position of having no idea what the *Cuneiform Records of Mesopotamia* actually are."

Rather to my surprise, Holmes did not tease or reproach me for the admission, but sought, in hushed tones, to provide me with a succinct explanation. "My dear friend, there is no shame in admitting that one lacks knowledge of such a specialist subject. In fact, there are only a handful of academics across the planet that have a full understanding of both the history and significance of cuneiform records. Around five thousand years ago, the Sumerian people of the Mesopotamian region developed an early form of writing which used pictures and symbols to convey information about their everyday social and economic affairs, like the harvesting of crops or the taxes that had to be paid by citizens. Through time, this developed into a more sophisticated script of signs and characters which we now call *cuneiform*. The ancient scribes used clay tablets on which to record their trade and community affairs and even chronicled their observations on astronomy. Their records and those of similar civilisations laid the very foundations on which many of today's Asian and Indo-European languages are based. For that reason, I have developed a fair working knowledge of cuneiform, but would not profess to be an expert by any means. Let us hope that our speaker can enlighten us further."

The lights in the reading room dimmed and the noise within the room subsided to a point where it would have been possible to hear a pin drop. A tall, frail looking man, with wire-framed glasses and a long black gown took to the stage. He was not quite the robust, middle-aged, archeologist I had envisaged Dr Canham-Page to be, and when he introduced himself, it was clear that I was not wrong. "Forgive me, gentlemen. I am Professor Michael Braydon of the Oxford University Archeology Faculty. It was to have been a great honour for me to be able to introduce to you this evening an esteemed colleague, arguably the very best archeologist that this country has ever produced..."

The professor paused at this point and looked visibly shaken. There were tears in his eyes and his hands, which were now firmly clutching the sides of the lectern, had begun to shake. With a deep breath he composed himself and continued. "There is no easy way to say this, but I am afraid that Dr Henry Canham-Page will not be able to speak to us this evening. Only a short while ago he collapsed in a back room of the library and my colleagues were unable to revive him. We have sent for a local doctor and the police, but it is clear that he has passed away."

There was a degree of pandemonium in the room as everyone began to talk at once with the shock of the announcement. Some attendees got up from their seats and began to saunter quietly towards the exits. Others looked almost angry at the news. A few were overcome with emotion and sat in a stunned silence.

No one seemed to notice the sad figure of Professor Braydon who appeared unable to release his grip on the lectern. In that moment, it was Holmes who stepped forward to assist the aged academic. With a word in his ear, he helped the professor down from the stage and nodded for me to join him. Against the backdrop of noise and confusion, Holmes explained that I was a doctor and could attend to the deceased. Braydon smiled weakly and led us off towards the back room where the earlier drama had occurred.

At the entrance to the room we were introduced to a man called Brendan Stevens, who explained that he was the manager responsible for organising the annual programme of academic lectures at the museum. He seemed relieved to hear that I was a doctor, but somewhat surprised to be introduced to Sherlock Holmes. "Mr Holmes, Dr Watson, this is indeed a pleasure - I just wish it were under more pleasant circumstances. Perhaps I ought to explain the sequence of events and why we felt it was necessary to call for the police in addition to a doctor."

Holmes was direct in his response. "Yes, Mr Stevens, I would be very grateful if you could outline the pertinent facts. I had already imagined that there might be some unusual or unexpected features when I first heard that the police had been called."

Stevens continued: "We had shown Dr Canham-Page to the room at about six o'clock this evening. All of our guest lecturers use the room before their talks. It gives them a quiet space in which to prepare themselves, which most seem to value. He had arrived by carriage and, I have to say, did look tired and despondent. I asked him if he wanted anything, like a glass of water or something to eat, but he indicated that he just wanted to be left alone and closed the door after I had left."

"That could be significant," mused Holmes.

"You will see when you enter the room that it is bereft of furniture. It has only a small desk and chair and no windows. In everyday use, it acts as a rest room for some of the museum staff. I was content to let the Doctor prepare in solitude, but around six thirty-five thought it wise to remind him of the time and check that he was not in need of anything for the lecture. Miss Prentice, one of our administrative staff, was with me. When we received no response to my knock, I entered the room and was shocked to see him lying on the floor close to the desk."

"I see. And has the furniture been moved at all since?"

"No, Mr Holmes. I busied myself checking his breathing and pulse and realised then that he was dead. I knew how important it would be to leave everything as it was. It seemed clear to me that he had died as a result of a blow to the back of his head. I could see and feel blood on the back of his skull, you see. What I did not know was whether the blow had been accidently or maliciously inflicted."

"Agreed. And no one has been in the room since?"

"That is correct. I instructed Miss Prentice to let Professor Braydon know what had happened and to call for a doctor and the police. She did so, and returned to the museum shortly before seven o'clock. Since that time, I have stood guard by the door."

Holmes was warm in his praise. "Thank you, Mr Stevens. Your summary and your actions to this point have been highly commendable. I think we should allow Dr Watson to take a look at the body now. He may be able to offer us some further insights on what may have led to the death."

As Holmes was about to turn the doorknob, a familiar voice rang out behind us. "Well, if it isn't my good friends, Sherlock Holmes and Dr Watson," cried Inspector Lestrade. "Now what brings you to these parts? Are you to tell me that there is some great mystery attached to this death?"

Holmes laughed. "Lestrade, my dear fellow. It is good to see you. And no, I am hoping that this will be a straightforward death. Watson and I were here for a lecture that the deceased was due to give this evening."

"I see. Well, let's have a look at what we're dealing with." He beckoned for Holmes to open the door.

When the three of us entered the room there was little to catch the eye beyond the outstretched body – feet towards us, face up and close to the desk in the left hand corner of the far wall. The room itself was about twelve feet square and the only other item in the space was a small wooden chair which was rested half way along the wall to our left. Holmes took a quick glance around the room and with his magnifying glass to hand began to scan areas of the floor along the left wall. At one point he stopped and using a small set of tweezers picked something from close to the wainscot and placed it in a matchbox he had retrieved from his pocket. Lestrade was content to stand back and allow Holmes to carry out his work. I knelt down and began to examine the body.

It was not difficult to determine how he had died. Dr Canham-Page had fallen back against the edge of the desk and cracked his head. His body lay twisted on the floor and from its position I imagined that his right arm and collarbone were likely to be broken. Underdoing a few of the studs on the front of his dress shirt enabled me to see that there was severe bruising all over his neck and upper arms consistent with a heavy fall. That left only one question – did he fall or was he pushed?

A cursory look over the rest of the body revealed only one other oddity. The archeologist appeared to be wearing black carpet slippers. Holmes had evidently noted my interest. "Yes, Watson. I also thought the footwear to be out of keeping with the formality of his evening attire; the dinner jacket, black trousers and bow tie. The other curious feature you may have noticed is that he still has in his right hand some rolled up sheets of foolscap – most likely the notes he planned to use for the lecture."

Lestrade interjected at this point. "Yes, Mr Holmes. That is most likely, as he does not seem to have brought anything else with him. If you look around the room, there is no case or bag of any kind."

"Quite so, Lestrade. But it would be as well to check his pockets." Holmes stooped to join me on the floor and began to search the pockets of the trousers, finding an assortment of coins and a set of keys. Retrieving only a small jar of pen ink from one of the two outside pockets of the jacket, he then turned his attention to the inside. From one of the hidden pockets he retrieved a black fountain pen, and from the other he pulled out a leather bound wallet, inside of which were two loose and separate pieces of paper.

"What have you found?" I asked.

"A wallet, containing...five pounds, a couple of Drury Lane theatre tickets and what looks like two notes or letters." He placed the wallet on the desk above us and scrutinised each note in turn. "Now, that is fascinating!"

Both Lestrade and I looked up keenly.

"We have one document which looks to contain a list of strange symbols and signs – probably one of the Doctor's academic pursuits. But the other document is more significant. At first glance, it appears to be a suicide note."

"A suicide note!" exclaimed Lestrade. "Now, I thought you said this wouldn't be an odd or unusual death, Mr Holmes."

"We will see, my friend. It suggests that there was some degree of mystery attached to this first document." He passed the note to Lestrade. "But the suicide note is addressed to a 'Dr Eversley', possibly one of Canham-Page's academic colleagues. In it he says, 'I know I can't go on like this. At times, the pain is just too acute.'" He passed the second document across to the inspector.

Lestrade studied both documents but looked confused. "Very strange, I'd say. But this list of hieroglyphics means nothing to me. And what does he mean when he talks about the 'first cuneiform'?"

I smiled and could not help interrupting. "A question similar to the one I asked of Holmes only half an hour ago, Inspector! Cuneiform is a type of symbolic alphabet I'm told."

There was a loud knock on the door and all three of us turned sharply. Brendan Stevens entered the room and announced, apologetically, that a local doctor had arrived to examine the body. Lestrade took it upon himself to leave the room and explain to the doctor that his services would not be required after all. While he was absent, Holmes was candid in his observations. "I do not know what conclusions you may have drawn, Doctor, but for me, the case seems straightforward until we get to the question of these two notes in the wallet."

I agreed wholeheartedly and added, "Yes, this does not strike me as any sort of suicide. It is quite clear that he cracked his head on the edge of the desk. There is a mark and a few strands of hair still on the desk to indicate where he fell and I would say that he has broken bones down his right side which suggest that he fell with some force. Do you think he could have been pushed?"

"Not a chance, Watson. You are right - he did fall heavily against the desk. In fact, he fell from the height of the chair. I would suggest that he lost his balance while on the chair and fell backwards."

"He was on the chair?" I asked incredulously.

"Yes, in the process of swatting a bee. Hence the reason he had his lecture notes rolled up in his hand. And it appears that he was successful." He withdrew from his pocket the

94

small matchbox he had used earlier. Inside I could see the crushed dead body of a honey bee.

"Remarkable! Perhaps he suffered from the effects of bee and wasp stings," I added. "I seem to remember that last year two physiologists, Paul Portier and Charles Richet, wrote papers describing the phenomenon of *anaphylaxis*, or the allergic - sometimes life-threatening - reaction that humans can have to foreign proteins they are exposed to. If he did suffer from it, his fear of bees would have been exaggerated. But why would he have fallen? He looks to have been physically fit and of no great age, and I am sure that his archaeological fieldwork would have kept him active. Would he really have lost his balance?"

Holmes was quick to respond. "Yes, Watson. All of what you say is likely to be true, but then you are forgetting the curious feature we both noted earlier."

"The carpet slippers?"

"Indeed. Now, why would he choose such footwear, not just to travel in, but to deliver a high profile public lecture?"

"It can only be for want of comfort," I replied, seeing where he was heading.

"Exactly! Now, let us examine his feet to see what may have been ailing him."

Responding to Holmes' lead, I knelt once more beside the body and carefully removed the black carpet slippers and the thin pair of black socks underneath. Looking at the two bare feet alongside each other, it was readily apparent that Dr Canham-Page did indeed have a foot condition. While his left foot showed no apparent deformities, the top of his right foot was swollen to an extent which rendered it much larger than the other.

95

"Interesting, Holmes. See the prominent bump along the top of the arch? Our man was suffering from *saddle bone deformity*. A condition caused by the excessive growth of bone material on the top of the foot. There is a gradual onset of the deformity which can afflict sufferers from their mid-twenties. Of itself, the condition does not produce much sensitivity, but the excessive rubbing of the skin on the top of stiff shoes would be extremely painful. Looking at the extent of this growth, I would say that Canham-Page has suffered with this for many years, and can only wear loose or soft-fitting footwear."

"So, potentially, the tightening of the slippers on his feet as he reached up and out to swing at the bee would have been excessively painful, causing his legs to buckle underneath him."

"I would say that is entirely possible."

At that point Lestrade re-entered the room and looked at us quizzically. "Now, now, Mr Holmes. You have that look on your face which suggests that you know something I don't. What have you discovered in my absence?"

Holmes chortled. "There is no keeping anything from you, Lestrade. I was just saying that I am firmly of the belief that this death was an accident. Dr Canham-Page appears to have fallen from the chair while in the process of killing a bee. Watson was suggesting that he may have had a deep-seated fear of bee stings and possibly even a severe medical reaction to them."

Lestrade looked unconvinced. "I see. But I thought we were talking about a possible suicide. What about this suicide note? It looks pretty convincing to me."

"Inspector, it strikes me that falling off a chair backwards in an attempt to hit one's head on the edge of a desk is just too far-fetched for anyone contemplating suicide. And as for the note, I think it has some other meaning or significance which has not yet become clear. I have studied the list of cuneiform symbols and the first in particular. I am not an expert, but this appears to be an obscure offshoot from the primary list of symbols developed over time by the Sumerian people. From the one or two symbols I do recognise, this looks to be a simple list of the key ingredients required for a good harvest – water, barley, long days and warm sunshine.

On listening to this my curiosity was aroused. "Could I see the notes?" I asked.

"Certainly," replied Lestrade, and passed both across to me. I laid them out on the desk. The first was the note containing the handwritten list of symbols. It read:

Ʊ Ŧ ѡ ≈ Ʌ Ӂ ≁ Д ѡ ‡

"I take it that this is Canham-Page's handwritten copy of some of the Mesopotamian cuneiform we would have heard about this evening?"

"Yes," said Holmes, "the ink is the same as that used on the supposed suicide note, which is actually signed by him and addressed to a Dr Eversley. It appears to make some reference to the first cuneiform symbol, as if that may have been some sort of key to unlock a wider academic mystery."

I turned my attention to the second note, again laying it out on the desk. This one read:

*Dear Dr Eversley,*

*I have checked the first cuneiform as you suggested, and it does appear to be the key to the mystery. I know I can't go*

*on like this. At times, the pain is just too acute. Action must
be taken.*

*Yours,*

*Dr Henry Canham-Page*

I smiled broadly as I read the note. "My dear Holmes. For
once, I think I can solve this particular mystery for you! This
is not a suicide note at all. I thought I recognised the name.
Dr Colin Eversley lives and works not half a mile from Baker
Street. He is a doctor, but not in an academic sense. Like me,
he is a medical practitioner. But, unlike me, he has chosen to
concentrate on a very specific area of treatment. Dr Eversley
is a chiropodist and has taken a lifelong interest in the
treatment of feet. Before his lecture this evening, Dr Canham-
Page had clearly penned a quick note to Eversley. The pain he
refers to is the result of his *saddle bone deformity* which has
got to the point where treatment is necessary. Dr Eversley
had obviously suggested a quick check prior to his client's
first consultation. If I tell you that the medical name for the
condition is *metatarsal cuneiform exostosis*, I think all will
become clear."

Holmes beamed at the pronouncement. "Watson, you have
excelled yourself! So, the 'first cuneiform' referred to has
nothing to do with the second note or any ancient
symbolism?"

"Nothing whatsoever. The medial cuneiform – also known as
the *first cuneiform* – is the largest of the foot bones. It is
situated at the medial side of the foot, to the front of the
navicular bone and at the base of the first metatarsal."

"Well I never! bellowed Lestrade. "So a case of bad feet
caused him to fall off a chair."

98

"So it would seem, Inspector - and no great mystery, after all. That said, I think Dr Watson deserves full credit. I was saying earlier that there is no shame in admitting to a lack of knowledge in a specialist subject. Watson's extensive medical training is way beyond my layman's understanding and has proved to be conclusive in this case."

"Hear, hear!" echoed Lestrade. "And thank you, gentlemen. Once again you have helped me to sort out what could have been a tricky case. I will explain to the library staff what has occurred and arrange for the body to be taken away. I am sorry you both missed out on your lecture this evening."

"There is no need to be concerned, Inspector. It is still early and I feel that Watson deserves a decent meal and a bottle of the finest red Bordeaux. I think we will therefore retire to the *Café Royal* for some French cuisine. If you are able to finish your shift at a reasonable time this evening, you are more than welcome to join us."

"That is kind of you, Mr Holmes, but I fear I have a long night ahead. Not that I will be having many more of those beyond this month. It seems only fair to tell you that I am retiring in a few days' time. I have been with Scotland Yard since I was sixteen and it is now time to call it a day. Mrs Lestrade and I have purchased a small cottage down in Kent, close to her relatives, so I think a country life beckons."

Both Holmes and I were surprised to hear the news, but pleased for the hard-working detective. We wished him the very best in his retirement and thanked him for his assistance in the many cases we had enjoyed together over two decades.

That evening, as we sat in the elegant interior of the *Café Royal*, Holmes proposed an unexpected toast. "To Inspector Lestrade – a fine officer and one who will be sorely missed."

I raised my glass at the worthy tribute. It was just another sign that time was marching on and none of us were getting any younger.

# 5. The Trimingham Escapade

Many of you will know that Sherlock Holmes lived out the final few years of his extraordinary existence well away from the hubbub of London and tending to his beloved bees on a quiet smallholding on the South Downs in Sussex. What is less well known is that he did, with occasional outbursts of energy and enthusiasm, continue to employ his talents on a small number of the more baffling and challenging criminal cases that were still being presented to him on a regular basis. One of these was a convoluted commission which Holmes took on in 1926 at the age of seventy-two. It was the last case we worked on together, so I have always looked on it with some affection. As such, it seems fitting that I should now record the details of what occurred that particular summer.

As had often been the case, my involvement in Holmes' investigation occurred more by accident than design. I had been visiting my dear friend on a radiant sunny day, having decided to take my new 3-litre Bentley touring car on its first excursion outside the capital. With little risk of rain and a full tank of petrol, I had cruised through the picturesque landscape of lowland heath, ancient woodlands and chalk grasslands to reach Holmes' modest farm near Saddlescombe in time for a light luncheon of salad and home-grown new potatoes.

Holmes was overjoyed at my visit, telling me about his new-found love of astronomy and his recent purchase of a powerful telescope, enabling him to explore for the first time the wonders of the solar system. Like a child with a new toy, he insisted on being taken for a spin in the Bentley and marvelled at its speed and comfort. I had rarely seen him more spirited. Yet, when we returned to the farm to find a black Austin Twelve parked outside his humble cottage, his countenance changed immediately.

"I fear our fraternal excitement is about to be rudely dampened by the long arm of the law, Watson. I recognise the number plate. It seems we have a visit from Chief Inspector Wattisfield of Scotland Yard - a capable fellow, but a man without humour. As you know, I have no telephone, so he has clearly made some effort to track me down. No doubt he has a perplexing case and is seeking some guidance. I hope you will linger a while longer and hear what the good man has to say?"

My response was immediate and heartfelt. "I wouldn't miss it for the world, Holmes!"

Wattisfield was brusque but amiable and, like Holmes, not one for irrelevancies and idle chit chat. When seated in Holmes' farmhouse kitchen, he went straight into the nature of his dilemma: "Mr Holmes. I have myself a very impenetrable murder mystery. Earlier this morning, we were called to Trimingham Manor in Surrey where the dead body of a solicitor named Barrington Henshaw was discovered in a locked room of the house. He appears to have fallen back against a stone fireplace and died of the head injuries he sustained. On the basis that the key to the room could not be found, I can only conclude that we are dealing with a case of potential murder or manslaughter. And given that we have not, as yet, ascertained the whereabouts of one of the household staff – a valet by the name of Heinz Descartes – I would suggest that he may have something to tell us about the nature of this unpleasant episode. We understand the man to be a German national, who has only recently come to this country, and I have alerted all ports and airports as to his identity to block any attempt he may make to escape to the continent."

Holmes was quick to pick up the baton. "Chief Inspector, I would be grateful if you could furnish me with some basic facts about the inhabitants of the house. I profess, I have never heard of Trimingham Manor."

The Chief Inspector nodded. "That does not surprise me, Mr Holmes. The house was restored only a few years back, when it was bought by David Harker, a wealthy gem dealer. He and his wife and child moved into the property in 1921 having previously lived in Holland. Sadly, both of the adults died earlier this year in a mining accident in South Africa, leaving their six-year-old son Gerald as the heir to the estate. It seems that Barrington Henshaw - legal advisor to the late David Harker - had been appointed as both the executor of his client's will and the legal guardian of young Gerald. Harker had left clear instructions that Henshaw was to find a good boarding school for the boy and to appoint a suitable personal valet for him at the earliest opportunity, to mentor his son during the school holidays when he returned home to the manor."

"The missing valet you referred to, I suppose?" said I.

"Yes, Doctor. Heinz Descartes was appointed in May this year. He had previously worked as some sort of butler at a French chateau, but hails originally from Hamburg. And by all accounts he was well-liked by young Harker and the two other inhabitants of the manor, Reggie and Elizabeth Dawson, gardener and housekeeper respectively. They had some admiration for the valet, who was described as being no older than about twenty-five years of age. He had doted on Gerald and, within a matter of weeks, they had seen a positive response from the boy, who once more had a smile on his face and was positive about the prospect of going off to boarding school."

Holmes raised an eyebrow. "I see. Well, perhaps we can return to Descartes a little later. What was your view of the Dawsons, Wattisfield?"

"Solid, dependable, working folk, Mr Holmes - came to work for Mr Harker with impeccable credentials. They had previously completed twenty years' unblemished service at the vicarage in Shalford, less than three miles from Trimingham. A couple in their mid-seventies, with three grown-up children, who are said to have been devastated by the loss of the Harkers and who have, according to the few neighbours that knew of the family, acted like grandparents to the boy. None too keen on the solicitor, Henshaw, though..."

"Really?" Holmes was quick to interpose. "So, what do we know about the dead man, I take it that he didn't live at the manor?"

"No, his legal practice was in Guildford and he originally acted for David Harker in the purchase of Trimingham. Lived in the village of Chilworth, a stone's throw from the manor and was well-known among the local hunting and shooting fraternity. Reggie Dawson suggested that Henshaw was a bit of a social climber. He was forty-two and engaged to be married to Verity Ainsworth, the wealthy and well-connected daughter of a local squire. With the appointment of the new valet, he had been spending less and less time at the house. But this morning he had arrived just before breakfast and came in through the back entrance."

"Something, I take it, that he hadn't done before, Wattisfield?" queried Holmes.

"Indeed. Mrs Dawson had just served Heinz Descartes a cooked breakfast and had earlier packed up a few sandwiches for Gerald Harker, who had gone off early by taxi to visit the new boarding school in Guildford which Mr Henshaw had arranged for him to attend. She was surprised to see Henshaw entering the back door to the kitchen with a briefcase, as it was his usual practice to drive up to the front entrance and enter the main door of the manor. He seemed flustered on seeing Mrs Dawson and asked hurriedly if he could join Mr Descartes for breakfast, having been told that the valet was still in the dining room, but planning to go out for a walk later that morning."

"And where was Mr Dawson at this time?" I enquired eager to know the whereabouts of all the key players.

"He had gone with Gerald to the boarding school. While Heinz Descartes had initially thought that he would accompany the boy in the taxi, Barrington Henshaw had asked specifically for Reggie Dawson to go with him, as he felt that the gardener's fatherly instincts might be better suited to the task."

"Well. We must now turn to the death itself, my good man. Perhaps you could outline the key facts as you see them?" asked Holmes.

The detective was keen to oblige and opened up his pocket book. "The room in question was used as a ground floor study by the late David Harker. Since his death, it has been kept locked, with Henshaw retaining the only key. The solicitor insisted on keeping the curtains to the room closed and would not allow anyone to enter the study. When he visited the manor he treated the room as his own, working at the desk and tapping away on a small typewriter he had brought with him from his office in Guildford. Mrs Dawson was not even permitted to clean the room."

"Very suggestive," mused Holmes, before nodding to encourage Wattisfield to continue with his narrative.

"At around eight-fifteen this morning, as Mrs Dawson was washing up the breakfast plates and cutlery, she heard the front door of the manor bang shut. Having come out into the hallway, she then watched through a window as Heinz Descartes ran off down the drive carrying a rucksack. At the time, she thought only that he must have been in a desperate hurry to get out for his walk, but was surprised, as she thought he had already left the house a short while earlier. She then remembered that she had not seen or heard Barrington Henshaw depart, so walked across to the door of the study and knocked as she always did when he was working. Getting no response, she tried the handle and found the door to be locked. By her own admission, she then knelt down and looked through the keyhole..."

I stifled a laugh at this point, bemused by the actions of the indomitable Mrs Dawson, as Holmes cast a disparaging glance in my direction. "Please carry on, Wattisfield, this is most enlightening," he intoned.

"...She realised that there was a light on in the room and was greeted with a dreadful sight. Through the spyhole she could see Henshaw lying on his back on the plush carpet, his feet pointed in her direction and his head close to the grate of the fireplace. She could also see a large pool of blood welled within the grate. Being alone and fearing the worst, she could see no way of breaking down the heavy oak door, so used the telephone in the hallway to call for both the police and an ambulance. A local constable arrived at the scene some fifteen minutes later, followed closely by an ambulance crew. Between them they used what tools they could find to take the door off its hinges and gain entry to the room."

Holmes cut in at this point. "And you said earlier that no key could be found?"

"That is correct. No key in the door or anywhere in the room, which suggests that it must have been locked from the outside. The local constable also did a quick search of Heinz Descartes' bedroom and was unable to find any such key."

Holmes responded a tad impatiently. "Quite so, Wattisfield. But what of this local constable? I trust he didn't start rearranging the furniture or tampering with the contents of either room?"

Wattisfield managed a strained smile. "You do not appear to have much faith in the modern police service, Mr Holmes. In point of fact, PC Curtis' conduct was exemplary. Having realised what he was dealing with, the young officer took every step to preserve the scene. His telephone call back to Surrey Police Headquarters prompted a request for Scotland Yard to be called in to assist. When I arrived at the manor close to midday, I found the diligent officer guarding the open entrance to the study."

"Splendid! My sincere apologies, Chief Inspector - you must realise that I have infrequent contact with many rural forces these days. I recognise that the police service must have moved on in leaps and bounds since the old days when Watson and I would often have cause to comment on the ineptitude of many a uniformed officer."

The detective shifted uneasily in the face of Holmes' barbed compliment, and returned to his notebook. "The manner of the death seems straightforward enough. Henshaw was well dressed in a tightly-cut tweed suit, white shirt and yellow tie. He appears to have cracked the back of his head on the fireplace as he fell. I travelled out to Trimingham with one of our pathologists, who insisted on having the body removed for further forensic examination. He persuaded the ambulance crew, who were still at the scene, to take him and the body back to London, although he did say he was fairly certain that it was the knock to the head which had killed Henshaw, rather than the blood loss. I can only apologise, Mr Holmes - I know that you would have preferred to see the body *in situ*."

I smiled instantly at the Chief Inspector's presumption that Holmes was likely to want to visit the scene any time soon.

"And we have still to ascertain whether he just fell in some way or was pushed. There were no obvious or visible signs of any assault on the body other than the head injury, so I retain an open mind on that one. But alongside the mystery of the locked door, we now come to the other fact which is baffling me, Mr Holmes. Prior to his death, Henshaw appeared to have been in the process of emptying a large quantity of cash from a hidden safe on the wall. Some of the money had been placed inside Henshaw's briefcase, which lay on the floor close to the desk, while the remainder lay in neat bundles within the safe. We have not, as yet, attempted to move or count the money, but I would say that it amounts to many thousands of pounds."

"Excellent!" exclaimed Holmes. "At last we are getting to the heart of this particular conundrum." His outburst surprised the Chief Inspector, who was momentarily lost for words.

"Does that mean you will be happy to assist us in our enquiries then, Mr Holmes? I confess to being at a loss to know how to proceed on this one. I feel certain that we can apprehend Mr Descartes at some point, but until we are able to question him, I fear we have little to go on."

Holmes was emphatic in his response. "Why yes - we would both be happy to take a trip across to the manor this afternoon, would we not, Watson? And as for further clues, I anticipate that we will discover lots more before we get any closer to finding the enigmatic Heinz Descartes. Time is of the essence, my good man, I have just to shut up my chickens and we can then make the trip to Trimingham."

*************************

As had happened so often in the past, Holmes had managed to get me embroiled in one of his cases against my better judgement. My plans to return to London that evening for a piano recital in Peckham were shelved instantly and I found myself wedged into the back seat of the police car, hurtling along tiny country lanes, listening to Holmes expound the virtues of home-reared pork over intensively-farmed pig meat. But it felt great to be back in his company on an active case which had so clearly stimulated his interest. After an hour or so, we were driving up the half-mile track which led us to Trimingham Manor.

The house itself was bigger than I imagined. Originally a Jacobean hall, Trimingham had been remodelled into a fine Edwardian-style property with attractive carved stonework, large family rooms and interior wood panelling. It was clear that David Harker had spent a lot of money restoring the home.

We had no sooner climbed from Wattisfield's vehicle when Holmes sprang to his feet, magnifying glass in hand, and proceeded to do a quick tour of the outside of the manor, pausing for some minutes to examine the two window frames of the study which was easily recognised, being the only downstairs room with its curtains drawn. Some five minutes later, Holmes returned to the bemused Chief Inspector and I, evidently pleased with what he had discovered.

"Worth a check - but I would say with some confidence, Wattisfield, that no one entered the study from outside the house, which suggests that if Henshaw had been attacked, his assailant had certainly been in the room before he arrived or had entered as Henshaw began to withdraw the cash from the safe."

After some introductions, we were admitted through the front door by the kindly Mrs Dawson. She had a warm, but commanding presence, and wore her dark grey hair up in a small bun. I imagined the housekeeper to be a resourceful woman perfectly suited to the role, although she looked as if the day's events had weighed heavily upon her mind. She was clearly tired and disconsolate and explained that her husband had returned, having been contacted by the police during the boarding school visit. In the circumstances, he had arranged for Gerald to stay overnight at the school. She went on to say that the gardener was currently tending to a broken fence at the back of the estate but could join us later if required.

Holmes looked particularly pleased to hear all of this and thanked her for the information. And as we continued to stand inside the large entrance hall, he asked a very direct question: "Mrs Dawson, what did you know about the Harker's financial affairs?"

The housekeeper seemed comfortable to answer openly, without hesitation. "Mr Harker was a cautious, but generous man, Mr Holmes. He was comfortable to spend money where it was required, on his family, the estate or any of the numerous charities he supported. He never talked to us about how he made his money and Reggie and I were never rude enough to ask him. He looked after us good and proper and made some specific provisions for us in his will. In short, we are to stay on in this house as paid employees until such a time as the Good Lord takes us."

"That is most gratifying to hear, Mrs Dawson. And was it Mr Henshaw who read the will?" asked Holmes.

"Yes. It was about a week or so after we learned about the death of Mr and Mrs Harker. And it was the last time that any of us set foot inside Mr Harker's study. Mr Henshaw called the two of us together with young Gerald and arranged some chairs around the desk, before announcing that he would read through the Harker's will. Insensitive man, he was. The mere mention of Gerald's parents brought the boy to tears, but Mr Henshaw just carried on in his usual abrupt manner."

"I see," said Holmes, "and what were the provisions of the will?"

"Well, beyond the bits that concerned the two of us, they were really quite simple. All of the estate and the Harkers' possessions were to pass to Gerald when he reached the age of eighteen. Nothing could be sold until such a time and Mr Henshaw was to act as legal guardian to the boy. A sum of money had been set aside to pay for the upkeep of the manor, Gerald's education and the recruitment of a personal valet. In total, Mr Henshaw said the estate had been valued at £115,000 and an additional sum of £15,000 had been deposited to cover all of the provisions I just mentioned."

"And do you know how the £15,000 has been deposited?" I asked for clarification.

"Yes. Mr Henshaw opened up a bank account for the money, which my husband and I control. It also receives deposits from some of the Harkers' other business interests and investments."

"That is very helpful – thank you, Mrs Dawson," Holmes said. The housekeeper looked relieved to be released from our scrutiny and headed off towards the back of the house, where I imagined the kitchen to be. The three of us then made our way across the large hall towards the open entrance of the study, the original door of which now lay propped up against a wall to the right. As we approached, a young police officer jumped up from a chair that had been placed to the left of the doorframe.

"PC Curtis, gentlemen," said the officer, standing to attention. His eyes darted from face to face, before settling on the famous consulting detective. "Very happy to be at your service, Mr Holmes," he said, "this is indeed an honour."

"Nonsense, Curtis, it is to you that we owe a debt of thanks, for having the good sense to preserve the scene." Holmes flashed a smile at Wattisfield, who remained impassive throughout the whole exchange. "And perhaps you could aid us further in our enquiries, young fellow?"

"Certainly, sir, in what way can I assist?"

"I would be grateful if you could take a short walk from the kitchen door and along the gravel path that leads off towards the back of the estate. I have already observed that the path ends at the edge of a small wood. We have been told by Mrs Dawson that beyond the copse her husband is in the process of mending a broken wooden fence. I would like you to find where he is working and locate a suitable point nearby where you can scale the fence, without causing any further damage. Within a short distance of that point you should see something which will confirm my working hypothesis."

Curtis seemed very relaxed about the task outlined, but Wattisfield shifted uneasily beside me. "Mr Holmes, I think the lad needs a little more direction than that. What exactly is he likely to see, assuming this theory of yours to be correct?"

A flash of irritation flickered across Holmes' face. "A car, Chief Inspector. To be precise, Barrington Henshaw's abandoned car. Did it not strike you as odd that having arrived at the house today, his car was nowhere to be seen?

112

Clearly he did not walk from his home, so his car must be somewhere. We learnt earlier that Henshaw had come into the house through the kitchen door, not the main entrance. It is my contention that he had hoped to enter the house without being seen by any of its occupants. He already knew that Mr Dawson and Gerald had gone off by taxi to the school and would have been able to watch from outside the house as Mrs Dawson served breakfast to Heinz Descartes. I have little doubt that he was heading for the study, in order to transfer the cash that was in the safe into his briefcase. I fully expect Curtis to find his car close to the broken boundary fence. I am working on the basis that that is where he climbed the fence, inadvertently breaking it as he did so."

"I see," replied Wattisfield. "Very clever, Mr Holmes. Let's hope you are right." He turned smartly towards PC Curtis. "Well, off you go lad - at the double!"

Curtis left us swiftly, heading off in the direction taken earlier by Mrs Dawson. The three of us then continued into the study. As Wattisfield and I stood back, just within the doorway, Holmes got to work. With his trusty magnifying glass he made a complete reconnaissance of the high-ceilinged study, pulling the curtains open slightly at one point to let in a shaft of sunlight, which immediately illuminated the open safe on the wall. From where I stood, I could see a considerable pile of banknotes still within the safe, each bundle wrapped around its middle by a white paper sheath. I imagined this was how they had been dispensed by the bank that had arranged for the sizeable cash withdrawal.

As Holmes went about his work, diligently and wholly preoccupied with the task at hand, my attention shifted towards the large fireplace in which Henshaw's body had been found. There was little doubt where the corpse had laid, a bright red halo of congealed blood still staining the hearth.

The mantelpiece against which he had fallen was made of Portland stone and appeared to be more decorative than functional. Positioned along it were a few photographs of what I took to be David Harker and his family.

Wattisfield followed my gaze and took it as a cue, opening his blue pocket book and sharing with us a few more details about the family based on his enquiries earlier that day.

"I'm told that Harker was originally from Maldon in Essex, where his family had built up a large and prosperous fishing business. But the family suffered such a string of accidents and deaths, that when David was born in 1897, he became, alongside his father, the only other surviving male member of the Harker family. When his parents both died in 1912, the fifteen-year-old inherited what remained of the fishing empire - two trawlers in desperate need of an overhaul. At the outbreak of the war, he sold the boats and became one of the first men in the town to volunteer, joining a company in the third battalion of The Essex Regiment in late 1915 and travelling out to France less than three months later."

"So, a fairly humble background for a man who went on to accumulate such a fortune," I observed.

"It would appear so, Dr Watson, and certainly not the sort of background that might have equipped him to pick up the trade of diamond dealing after the war. Mrs Dawson said that Harker had once confided in her that until he made the first trip to Trimingham Manor after its purchase, he had not once returned to England since first setting off from his East Anglian home to fight on the Western Front. She had also never known Harker to receive any family guests at the manor."

"Do you know anything further about his war record, Chief Inspector?"

"Well, only what I could glean from a telephone call to an old service colleague at the War Office. He told me that Harker's Essex battalion had entered the fighting during the Battle of the Somme in 1916, and that his company had all but been wiped out – in fact, only four soldiers had survived the campaign. These were a Sergeant Geoff Simkins and three privates, one of whom was Harker. All had been decorated for their bravery. Under Simkins' supervision, the four had then been assigned to a motorised division and engaged in running supplies to the front. This they had continued to do until May 1917, when their two trucks had been attacked and destroyed by the Germans near Bullecourt, on the journey to Arras in France. Despite the attack, Simkins and Harker had apparently survived, but were destined never to see each other again. And here we have another mystery..."

As busy as he was, crawling around on the carpet and checking desk drawers, I had imagined Holmes to be completely oblivious to anything Wattisfield had relayed to this point. But on hearing the word 'mystery', Holmes piped up suddenly. "My dear Chief Inspector, I fear you may have been unduly economical in sharing with us earlier the key facts of this case. I'm at once intrigued to hear more of these revelations about Harker's past as I believe them to be central to the events which unfolded here this very morning. Please enlighten us..."

"Well, the official records show that Sergeant Simpkins was taken by the Germans and held as a prisoner of war until 1918, after which he returned home to his wife and family in Harwich - two stone lighter, but otherwise fit and healthy. In comparison, one day after the fateful attack near Bullecourt, Private David Harker had presented himself to a Major Williams at the British position near Arras. He sketched out what had happened during the attack and explained that he was the only survivor from his original company. He indicated that he had walked from Bullecourt to reach Arras. After a couple of days recuperating, Harker had joined a new company and was moved to Piave in Italy. From that point on, he fought in a variety of places until spring 1918, when he was transferred back to the Western Front. Just before the war ended, he was engaged in moving food and other supplies into Holland. The records suggest that Harker had never returned from Holland."

I could not at this juncture see any great mystery in what the Chief Inspector had outlined, and voiced my concern. He was quick to respond.

"Agreed - in itself, there appears to be nothing particularly remarkable about Harker's movements. The real mystery lies not with that, but in the observations that Simkins made on his release from the prisoner of war camp in 1918. In providing the War Office with a full account of his capture, he was adamant that he had been the only survivor of the German attack. He said that he had seen Harker die that day and when shown a photograph of the Essex man - taken at the time Harker was transferred to his new company in Italy - Simkins was on record as saying that the person in the photograph bore no resemblance whatsoever to the soldier he had served with."

"Very enlightening," said Holmes. "And what did the authorities do as a result of this claim?"

"Nothing, apparently. Harker had already been demobbed at that point and was residing somewhere in Holland. I imagine the War Office had more pressing concerns to deal with, so let the matter rest there."

"And what of Harker after the war? Do you have anything more you can tell us about that?"

Wattisfield flicked forward in his notebook. "Only a few bits and pieces which Mr and Mrs Dawson shared with me, based on their conversations with the Harkers. They understood that after the war, Harker had continued to live in the Dutch town of Giethoorn in the Eastern Province of Overrijssel, where he married a local girl called Katerina. In 1920, their son Gerald was born. Harker was said to be well regarded in the town, making a modest living as a gem dealer. A year later, he bought Trimingham Manor and moved the family to England. He continued to have a number of business ventures in Holland and beyond, including a controlling interest in some diamond mines in South Africa. Earlier this year, he and Katerina had been invited to tour one of the newly-opened mines in the Archaean Witwatersrand Basin. As they did so, a pocket of trapped gas was ignited by a miner's candle lamp and the explosion ripped through the mineshaft, trapping the touring party and killing the couple. As the appointed executor of their legal and financial affairs, Barrington Henshaw took charge of everything from that point on."

"I must commend you for your thoroughness, Chief Inspector. That you have managed to ascertain all of that background information in just a few short hours is indeed testament to your professionalism," observed my friend.

"Thank you, Mr Holmes, but I fear it has done little to help me solve this particular mystery. I am still no closer to understanding why Heinz Descartes may have attacked Henshaw or, indeed, what any of this has to do with the money in the safe."

Holmes smiled at the detective. "I may have a few more observations to add to our existing knowledge. And, unless I am very much mistaken, young Curtis is about to re-join us and tell us all about his findings."

The footsteps from the hallway drew nearer and PC Curtis entered the study a couple of seconds later. He was red in the face and a thin sheen of sweat clung to his forehead - clearly not the sort of day to be running around in a heavy police uniform. "As you rightly guessed, Mr Holmes, there is a car parked in a clearing among some elms which back on to the fence at the rear of the estate. The new-style tax disk gave no hint as to the car's owner, but on the front passenger seat were some papers, headed up with the words 'Henshaw Legal Services'."

"Capital! I will forgive you for your suggestion that I merely guessed at the location of the car, PC Curtis, when it was in many ways the only feasible explanation for what had happened to Henshaw's vehicle, but then I digress. I was about to share some other observations on what occurred within this house earlier today."

PC Curtis looked suitably admonished, but when I cast a glance in Wattisfield's direction, I saw him give the young officer a sly wink of approval. Holmes seemed not to notice and carried on with his deliberations.

"Heinz Descartes had already informed Henshaw that he was to take a walk around the estate after his cooked breakfast. Having left Henshaw at the dining table, he returned briefly to his room, to pick up his rucksack and, no doubt, a few provisions for his hike. I think it unlikely that he would have taken the rucksack down to breakfast with him. Having collected this, he then left the manor and began to walk off down the drive. However, he retraced his steps back to the house only a short while later, perhaps to retrieve something he had forgotten or to spy on the movements of Henshaw. Either way, Mrs Dawson was not wrong in her assertion that Descartes had left the house twice this morning. For his part, I imagine Henshaw had left the breakfast table as soon as

Descartes was out of earshot and had made for the study, fully intent on emptying the money from the safe, while all of the other occupants were busy."

"What motive do you imagine he had for taking the money, Mr Holmes, was it just greed – a simple matter of theft?" asked Wattisfield.

"In this case, I believe it was simply that, Chief Inspector. With his impending wedding to the wealthy socialite, Verity Ainsworth, we can surmise only that he needed to supplement his solicitor's salary with some extra funds. However, I am certain that he was the only person alive who knew the cash was in the hidden safe – it was originally a nest egg of Harker's. In the reading of the will, there was no mention of the extra cash, which makes me believe that Harker had been content for the money to be secreted in the safe for some purpose other than the general maintenance of his family or the running of the estate. With Harker dead, Henshaw hoped to take the money for his own purposes."

"If that was the case, why did Henshaw not take the money earlier, Holmes," I enquired.

"A good question. But this is where our friend Descartes comes into the story. I am inclined to believe that it was no accident that the German arrived at Trimingham Manor looking for work soon after the Harkers had died. A search of his room a little later should confirm my thoughts on that. For the moment, let us assume that with the unexpected arrival of Mr Descartes, Henshaw was forced to put his plans on hold, until he could find a suitable opportunity to retrieve the money from the safe."

"So, are you saying that Descartes knew about the money then, Mr Holmes?" asked Curtis, clearly keen to make sense of the story as we all were. "It's just that I thought you said earlier that only Henshaw knew about the contents of the safe."

"Yes, Curtis. I am certain that Descartes knew about the money, he just didn't know *where* it was. Only Henshaw knew about the hidden safe and he retained the key to open it. Descartes cannot have been immune to the fact that no one other than the solicitor was allowed in the room. Perhaps that is why he came back to the manor, to see what Henshaw was up to."

Wattisfield was the next to comment. "Working along the lines of your theory then, Mr Holmes, we have Descartes returning to the house and catching Henshaw in the act of taking the money from the safe. An altercation then takes place as a result of this, and Henshaw is either pushed, or falls back accidently, against the mantelpiece..."

"Quite so, my friend. We are indeed fortunate that Henshaw took to keeping the door of the study locked and the room out of reach of Mrs Dawson and her excellent cleaning regime - I have rarely seen a more pristinely maintained domestic interior than the area outside of this room. But, with the curtains opened up a fraction, you will observe that we have a revealing layer of fine dust on all of the furniture surfaces. Look closely at the desk top and you will discern that we have preserved a small record of what occurred between Descartes and Henshaw in the moments before the latter's demise."

Holmes then walked around the desk and positioned himself to one side of the heavy oak bureau, with the fireplace behind him. "Henshaw would have stood somewhere around here. And as Descartes moved towards him, or wrestled with him, we can see how Henshaw's hand swept back over the desktop leaving a distinct trail in the dust. The fingerprints at the edge of the desk are where he tried in vain to cling to the woodwork before falling backwards."

Wattisfield continued to look unconvinced: "So, Descartes then makes off from the scene, carrying only the possessions he has with him. There is, of course, one obvious flaw in this *imagined chain of events...*"

"And that is, Chief Inspector?"

"Well, if Descartes knew of the money as you suggest and had come to Trimingham because of it, he missed an obvious opportunity. All of us can see that theft was clearly not his game plan, as the money is still in the safe."

Holmes was quick to chide the officer. "What we see and what we deduce from those observations are two different matters. I am convinced that Descartes was motivated to take only a proportion of the money – possibly an amount that he had been told was his or that he believed he was entitled to. Either way, he took £40,000 in cash, no more, no less."

PC Curtis let out a whistle. "That's a tidy sum, I'd say, Mr Holmes. But how do you know how much he took?"

"He took exactly half of what was in the safe. If you examine each of the bundles of banknotes, you will see that the individual serial numbers run in a consecutive sequence, indicating that they were withdrawn in one batch as brand new currency. Luckily for us, Descartes drew his share from half of what was in the safe, ignoring those notes which Henshaw had already placed in the briefcase. In effect, he took a portion of banknotes from the middle of the consecutive sequence. Taking the first serial number - which is in one of the bundles in the case – and the last, which still sits in the safe, we can calculate that the total haul was worth £80,000. Counting up what is in the safe and the briefcase indicates that just half of that amount remains. A simple matter of mathematics."

Wattisfield looked impressed at last. "Mr Holmes, my apologies. I knew that you would be the man for this job. That is a very neat piece of deduction, I must say."

Holmes swept aside the compliment. "We still have a few dots to join up I fear. Would it now be possible to have a look at Heinz Descartes' room?"

"Certainly, Mr Holmes. Perhaps I can ask PC Curtis to take you up there this instant. Not that you'll see much – Descartes has very few possessions and clearly brought little with him when he travelled to England. You must excuse me for a few moments. I have to put in a quick telephone call to Scotland Yard to check on progress elsewhere."

We were led up the grand stairway of the manor house and into the rooms and chambers of the first floor, where Heinz Descartes' bedroom was situated towards the back of the house. Entering the room, I could see that it was indeed sparsely furnished. In addition to a small single bed, table and armoire, I could see only one other piece of furniture – a small walnut bureau decorated with scarlet and gilt inlays.

Holmes headed immediately for the piece without even bothering to check the drawer of the table or corner armoire. I recognised the gleam in his eye, the traditional fervour and thrill of the chase that he had always displayed on our earlier Baker Street adventures. Seconds later, he was lifting the box, examining its sides, checking for drawers and probing its operation. With two faint clicks, he had removed an interior veneered panel to reveal a hidden recess from which he pulled a folded document. PC Curtis and I looked on in astonishment.

"By God, Holmes!" I gasped. "How could you possibly have known that you would find that?"

"A hunch, my dear Watson, but a strong one. I was always convinced that Descartes came here with the knowledge that some money awaited him. There had to be some documentary evidence for that, something he could refer to, to prove his claim. A document that he would, quite naturally, wish to keep hidden, until asked to verify the claim. Where better to hide such a document than in this – what looks like his only personal possession. And one which he had no opportunity to retrieve this morning in his haste to escape from the manor after his altercation with Henshaw."

He opened out the papers onto his lap and scanned the first and last page of the document. His facial expression remained unchanged, giving little away. In fact, the absence of any reaction meant that I was unprepared for what he then went on to reveal. A moment later, he observed, rather casually: "This appears to be a letter from David Harker to Heinz Descartes, written from this manor in the summer of 1921, just after Harker had moved into his new home. Out of courtesy, we will await the return of Chief Inspector Wattisfield. We should then be ready to hear what brought Mr Descartes to these rural shires."

Wattisfield did not keep us waiting long, but the anticipation of what we might find had Curtis and I speculating wildly about the contents of the letter. As ever, Holmes remained impassive and impervious to our banter.

"Gentlemen, you must forgive me," exclaimed the Chief Inspector, on entering the room, "but I have good news! The pathologist has confirmed that the cause of death was indeed the blow to the head – the trauma of which is consistent with a fall against something like a mantelpiece. He could find no other significant marks on the body to indicate that an assault had taken place, so we may be looking at a case of manslaughter rather than murder. But the real news is that

Heinz Descartes has been arrested this afternoon at a boarding house in Poole. He is being held overnight at a local police station in the town. It should therefore be only a small matter of time before we can put our questions directly to him, Mr Holmes, and resolve this matter once and for all."

Holmes was quick to praise the police effort. "My dear fellow, that is tremendous news. Let us hope that Descartes is forthcoming in his answers. While you were making your calls, we were also making very good progress," said he, holding up the letter with just a hint of glee. "It appears that we may already have some answers within this document, which was secreted within Descartes' *bonheur-du-jour*."

The Chief Inspector could hardly contain his joy. "Perhaps then, we should retire to the drawing room, gentlemen. And I will see if I can prevail on the goodly Mrs Dawson to provide us with a small brandy or whisky to accompany your recitation, Mr Holmes."

\*\*\*\*\*\*\*\*\*\*\*\*\*\*\*\*\*\*\*\*\*\*\*\*

Some ten minutes later, we were all seated in the dining room, with glasses and cigars to hand. Holmes then read the letter as follows:

*Trimingham Manor*
*Guildford*
*Surrey*
*England*

*18th August, 1921*

*Dear Heinrich,*

*You will have to forgive me for the fact that I am communicating with you by letter rather than face to face. I am also very sorry to have to write this to you in English, but whilst I have some mastery of both the French and Dutch languages, I cannot claim to be fluent in German. All will become clearer as I proceed.*

*This is not an easy letter for me to write. It concerns both of our pasts and, significantly, our futures too. I have thought long and hard about how I would set the facts down on paper and have concluded that I can but tell the truth as I see it. There appears to be no other way. As such, this letter is as much a confession on my part as it is an explanation to you. When you have read this, you will know more about my past than any other person alive, including those nearest and dearest to me. I hope that the facts will remain known only to the two of us.*

*I will try not to bore you with irrelevancies, but do need to delve sometime back into the past.*

*I was born in the English village of Cratfield in Suffolk in the early winter of 1900, one of two brothers from an established farming family. From an early age I think I knew that my destiny would have little to do with the family business. In any case, my brother, Tom Coleman, being the eldest by one year, was set to inherit the farm and all of our land, so there was always a general expectation that I, Peter Coleman, would have to make a life of my own. From an early age I read and dreamt of travelling and was hungry to learn more about the world outside of our small village.*

*With the war in 1914, our lives were turned upside down and steadily we watched as increasing numbers of our friends and relatives went off to fight on the Western Front. I imagine your memories of that time are no less frightening. Working on the farm, Tom and I had plenty to keep us busy and I have to say that neither of us had any great desire to join the army – in any case, I was still too young.*

125

From the early part of 1916, we faced a more immediate threat to our safety. Zeppelin airships began to attack the eastern coastline with frightening regularity, bombing coastal ports and towns and terrifying the local population. You will understand that we were not used to such attacks and were unprepared for the war to be brought to the doorsteps of our homes and farms. In fact, I am sure that the fear of those attacks was generally much worse than any actual damage the airships inflicted.

It was during one of those early airship raids that my story really begins.

I was woken in the early hours of 12th August, 1916 by the familiar sound of artillery guns further down the coast. Instinctively, I ran to my bedroom window and looking skyward saw a continuous tornado of shells being sent up against what I imagined to be a German raiding party. Searchlights from the ground were moving across the sky trying to locate the attackers and at one point I saw the lights catch and hold a Zeppelin in their grasp. I could hear the sound of the airship's engines droning high above. All the while, the guns continued to pound. For whatever reason, I decided to dress and go outside.

Out in the cold air, I watched as the Zeppelin continued across the sky, tracked by the searchlights, and visible in the growing dawn of the new day. I had made my way down through some woodland about a mile from our farmhouse and pulled myself up onto a wooden gate. At this point, the guns fell silent and I could see the lights of three or four aircraft rising up to attack the airship that, by this time, had shut down its engines and appeared to be drifting out of control towards the coast. The aircraft began to attack the Zeppelin, the rapid bursts of their machine guns being clearly audible from where I sat.

*As I watched the events unfold, I was startled to see and hear an explosion at the rear end of the airship. Bright orange flames began to appear above the tail of the craft, moving steadily forwards towards its nose. You might think that I would have felt some joy at seeing the destruction of this hostile invader, but I can say that I felt only horror at the thought of the airmen trapped aboard her flaming hulk. I could hardly bear to watch as the airship dipped at the rear and began to fall to earth. But it was then that my fears become more acute. Over the course of the next five minutes, I watched as the ship fell closer and closer towards our land.*

*As the Zeppelin fell, I could see a tall column of fire stretching up above her and a long trail of black smoke tracing out her descent. Getting ever closer and nearing the ground, I watched as the stricken craft barely cleared the woods to my side and passed overhead, showering hot debris throughout the trees and across the open field ahead. I remained fixed to the gate, too terrified to move. At less than one hundred feet from the ground, I saw what I thought were black bombs being launched from the airship, but as I watched and waited for the explosions, I realised to my horror that these missiles were in fact the bodies of some of the crew jumping or falling into the field. At that point, the Zeppelin hit the ground with a tremendous bumping, grinding and twisting of metal and continued to travel across the ploughed soil before coming to an abrupt halt on the far side of the field. A large explosion followed and numerous fires across the site flared up and continued unabated.*

*I could go on at length to tell you about the aftermath of the crash and the efforts made by countless Englishmen to save the few crewmen that remained alive in the burning debris. To explain how the crash site attracted thrill-seekers from far and wide and to commiserate with you about the fact that in the end, all nineteen German airmen lost their lives in this tragic episode. No doubt you will know much of this, and I imagine you will already have guessed how you are linked to the story. But there is much, much more, to tell.*

*For the two hours immediately following the crash, most attention was focused on the field where the Zeppelin came to rest. All but one of the crew died there, having burned to death in the craft or having fallen from the airship before it crashed. The one crewmember not found there had jumped from his position in the rear engine car of the airship as it passed over the woods adjoining our farmland. He had been spared the agony of burning to death, but as he fell through the trees at speed had broken numerous bones in his body, including his neck. He lived for an hour after the crash before being found by an English Army doctor. I know this because I spent those last precious moments with him, comforting him as he passed away. You need to know this, because he was your father, Franz George Descartes.*

*I appreciate that it may be difficult for you to come to terms with all that I am about to tell you, but you must bear with me. Franz would have wanted it that way – he told me so.*

*I did not move from the wooden gate until the airship had hit the ground. At that point, I realised that I must get help. In fact, I need not have worried as within minutes people from the village began to arrive at the scene, running across the field towards the burning ship. As I jumped down from the gate intending to follow the others, I heard a voice from the woods nearby. I climbed back over the gate and proceeded into the trees, following the sound. I could catch only odd words as I stumbled through the semi-lit woodland, but recognised that those words were in German.*

*When I finally reached Franz, he lay on his back as if sleeping. As I stood above him, unsure what to do next, he* smiled up at me and said in perfect English, "Please do not be afraid, my friend, you can see that I am in no position to hurt you!"

I was surprised by the calmness in his voice, as I could already see that he was unable to move his limbs and must have been in tremendous pain. "Please, sit beside me," he continued. "I may have only a short time to live and have much to say. What is your name? Please, do not worry about getting me any food or water, it will only waste time."

I told him who I was and how I had watched the airship descend. He then asked me if any of the others had survived the crash and I told him that I thought it unlikely. He appeared to be upset by this and fell silent for a few moments. I asked him where he came from in Germany and he told me that he lived in Hamburg with his wife Gretel and young son, Heinrich. He seemed pleased that I had asked him about his homeland and said that his family meant more to him than anything else in the world. It was for this reason that he needed to talk and he asked only that I listen to what he had to say. I was in no position to argue, and my only fear was that we would be discovered before he was able to finish what he had to say. I then sat beside him and listened intently to every word he uttered.

Let me begin by saying that Franz was an incredible narrator. Even in that final hour, suffering untold pain, he was able to tell his story with colour and vivacity. And in those passing moments, I think he recognised in me a yearning for adventure and an eagerness to hear all that he had to say about parts of the world I had yet to explore. I have never been a deeply religious man, but I have always thought that there was a degree of predetermination in the way that our lives were brought together that fateful morning.

*Franz explained that he had been born in France in 1880, the only son of Jean Descartes, a wealthy diamond merchant. His family moved around Europe at frequent intervals and by the time he was eight years of age, the young Franz could speak excellent English, German and Spanish, alongside his native French. However, as a result of his father's declining health, the family finally settled in a large house in the provincial French town of Albert during the summer of 1890. Franz loved the house, with its elegant blue façade and the line of topiary trees that stood in large pots along the front of the building. And he had fond memories of the countryside throughout the Picardie Region of Northern France.*

*Within six months his father died, leaving the family with some assets, but some even larger debts. Franz' grief-stricken mother, Karin - a German by birth - could not understand how the family could be left in such a position given Jean's lifetime of successful business dealings. But, in short, she was forced to accept the situation, selling the townhouse less than a year later to pay off their debts and moving with Franz back to her hometown of Mansell on the banks of Lake Constance in Southern Germany.*

*All of this was stressful enough to Franz, but on his sixteenth birthday he received a mysterious package from a firm of solicitors in France that Jean Descartes had always turned to for legal advice. On opening the package, he found that it contained a small key and a letter written to him by his father. Jean had written the letter on his deathbed, without the knowledge of Karin, and had arranged for it to be sent by the firm after his death. Urging Franz to ensure that the letter did not fall into anyone's hands but his own, he went on to explain that over the years he had accumulated a fortune in diamonds, which he always planned to live off in his old age and to pass on to his family. However, his health had worked against him and so he found himself in the position where he had to think only of the family he would leave behind. But herein lay a problem.*

*Jean had known for some time that Karin Descartes had a lover, the 28-year-old Mayor of the town. At first, he had ignored their liaisons, hoping that the relationship would not develop into anything serious. He explained to the stunned Franz that their marriage had been loveless for a number of years, so he had always feared a situation like this. Karin had not been prepared to give up her lover and the relationship had become public knowledge throughout the town, much to Jean's distress and contributing to his ill health. As a result, he determined that whilst Franz should inherit what was rightfully his, he would not leave more than an adequate amount to his widow. In any case, Jean knew that Karin's rich family back in Mansell would never see her fall on hard times.*

*Jean Descartes had struggled to think of a way of preserving Franz' birthright without involving Karin and avoiding a complex legal process. He felt certain that any legal resolution would be challenged by lawyers working for Karin's family. This he could not risk. But he did, finally, engineer a solution. He explained that he had withdrawn from the security of numerous bank vaults, his full supply of diamonds and had placed them within a locked safe built into one of the interior walls of the French town house. This had been bricked over and the whole plan had been executed in secret when Karin and Franz had been away for a week in Paris. Franz now held the only key to that safe and Jean wished him every success and happiness in his life ahead.*

*Franz could barely take all of this in, as he read the letter in the drawing room of his new home in Mansell. Without his mother's assistance he had no way of getting back to France and even if he could, had no idea how he could locate the safe and liberate its contents. And, to make matters worse, Karin Descartes herself died in a boating accident in 1897. In her written will, Franz learned that she had left all of her wealth to her relatives in Mansell, as she had it "...on good authority that my late husband has provided for our son, Franz, in some manner which he has not seen fit to share with me." Franz felt betrayed.*

*Penniless and estranged from his mother's family, Franz joined the Naval Reserve and began to train as an engineer in the Imperial shipyards in Kiel. Immersing himself in his work, he tried to forget about the diamonds and his parents. He enjoyed the work and was well regarded by his employers. In 1899, he married your mother, Nicole - a dark-haired, blue-eyed girl from Munich – and the pair moved to Hamburg. And, in April 1900, you were born to them, Heinrich.*

*Your father made it clear to me that you and your mother were always the primary focus of his life. But at intervals, he thought about the diamonds back in Albert and kept the small key to the safe within a specially fashioned locket around his neck. He even arranged for copies of the town's local newspaper to be sent to him in Germany, feeling certain that if the diamonds were ever discovered he would be able to find out and put in a claim for them. But he heard nothing.*

*The years passed steadily, but with the outbreak of war, Franz was drafted into the Naval Airship Division of the German Fleet Command and became a Stoker Petty Officer on board a Zeppelin airship. Seeing less and less of his family, and risking his life during every air raid over England, he promised himself that when the war was over he would travel to France and reclaim the diamonds for you all to enjoy.*

*Such was Franz' story, told to me that morning as he lay dying in an English wood, far from his family. He had told me the story because he needed to tell someone – anyone - before he died. "I am not sure why I have told you all of this, Peter," he said, looking suddenly tired and weak, "but you are a good listener. I have only one further request of you, and that is that you get a message to my wife and son to say that I love them both and regret that I cannot be with them. Please tell Heinrich that his father was very proud of him."*

*I was deeply moved by Franz' words as the life began to drain from him. I had only known this man for less than an hour in the most surreal of circumstances, but I already knew that I felt closer to him than almost anyone I had ever met. "What about the diamonds?" I enquired, "...is there no way that Heinrich can claim them for himself?"*

*"I doubt it," he replied quietly. "I have never told Nicole or Heinrich about the diamonds. You are the only person who knows about them besides me."*

*"What about if I help? I could let Heinrich know the story. He could travel to France when he is older, find the townhouse and get the diamonds. Surely there is hope," I said in desperation.*

*Franz looked at me wearily. "My friend, you forget that we are at war. Whilst I am French by birth, my son is German. Even if the war were to end soon, I cannot imagine that he would be welcomed, open-armed, by the people of Albert. They would hardly be placated by the knowledge that he was the son of Franz Descartes, who went off to live in Germany and became a Zeppelin raider. Those with long memories will know that Madame Descartes brought shame* to the town by her scandalous affair with the Mayor. In any case, what right would he have to enter the house and break down the walls in search of the safe?"

In that moment I knew that I could not leave your father to die without hope. I told him that I would make contact with his family and pass on his final words. But I found myself going further, desperate to help this dying man - a stranger and an enemy of my country. "What if I find the diamonds and deliver Heinrich's birthright to him?" I ventured.

Franz fixed his gaze on me, staring intently for what seemed like an eternity. Eventually he replied. "You cannot know what you are taking on, Peter. I am guessing that you have never travelled more than fifty miles from your farm. What do you know of the world? How would you do all of this? And why would you bother? I am dying. I have achieved what I wanted – all that I ask is that you pass on my last words to my family. I can ask nothing further. Please leave me now."

I felt hurt by his rebuke, but was not prepared to give up. "As I see it, you have no choice. I will make contact with your family, but sometime in the future I will also try to find the diamonds and ensure that your family receive what is rightfully theirs."

He winced in pain and for the first time I could see tears in his eyes. Away in the distance I could hear voices, English voices, getting ever closer in the morning light. "You are right," he said at last, "I have no choice, I am a dead man. But I will make you promise me this. Should you find the diamonds and carry out your plan, you must promise me that you will sell the gems and take half of the proceeds."

I began to interject, but he silenced me abruptly. "You must promise me this, Peter. It is my will. I want you to take half.

*It is only fair. It is more than I could ask of you and more than I could imagine at this time. But there is something more that you must have."*

*He smiled at me and his pained eyes looked down at his chest. "The key, Peter, you must take the safe key. It is in the locket around my neck. Now take it and promise me that you will honour my wishes."*

*I hesitated at this point. But watching his eyes and mouth close slowly, I realised that his time had come. I opened his large, fur-lined overcoat and undid the silver buttons at the neck of his uniform. My hand felt for the chain around his neck and slowly I pulled out a small decorative locket with a crucifix on its lid. Opening the clasp, I pulled out a small, dark-metal key and placed this in my pocket. On the inside lid of the locket I could see a small picture of what I guessed to be you and your mother. I closed the locket and once again placed it beneath his clothes. His eyes opened briefly and finally. I found myself whispering to him, as if somehow disturbing his sleep. "I won't let you down."*

*I stood up at this point and thought I saw him smile, but realised then that he was dead. Behind me, I heard a voice cry out. I turned and saw a uniformed officer running towards me. As he reached us, I saw him look me over before glancing down at Franz. "I'm Major Davenport, Royal Army Medical Corps. Is he dead?"*

*"Yes, he's dead," I answered, and struggled to hold back the tears.*

*The Major looked at me sympathetically. "Don't worry, son, happens to us all - both the death and the grieving. Never an easy thing to see someone die, even your enemies."*

*There was much activity after that. Throughout the day various branches of the military came and went and a massive clear up operation began. I was questioned by an Army Captain, but maintained that I had run from the farmhouse after the crash and had only ventured into the woods a short time before Major Davenport had found me. All of which seemed highly plausible.*

*Ten days later, the crew were buried in the village churchyard, the event being attended by around 300 local people and army and navy personnel. It was a simple ceremony, with due respect given to the German airmen, in spite of the inevitable and popular hostility that many of the villagers had towards these raiders.*

*We were told that where any personal belongings had been found near the crash site, these would be returned to the families of the dead. I have always hoped that this was the case. In fact, if you do have in your possession the locket that Franz wore, you will now know for certain that what I have told you is the truth. All of which would be enough of a story. But I still have much more to tell.*

*For the next two months, I could think of nothing else but Franz and his legacy. My brother noticed the change in me. He said that I had grown up in a short space of time. He knew that the crash had had a big impact on me, but clearly did not know why. I confided in him that I needed to get away from the farm and travel. We both knew what that meant. In short, I told him that I was going to join the army and fight in France. He tried to talk me out of it and pointed out that I was still too young. But I would not listen and said that I would lie about my age. I was a tall lad anyway and the years of farm labour had built me up to look much older than I was.*

*I remained resolute in my determination to travel to France and do what I had agreed to. I managed to find out some information about the town of Albert and committed this to memory. Joining the army seemed the only option, although I had no idea what I would do if I ever made it onto French soil. Using some money given to me by Tom, I travelled to Ipswich one Saturday morning and, lying about my age, joined the armed forces. After a period of training in England, I was taken along with countless other young men across to France to face the horrors of the Western Front.*

*In many respects, I could not have joined the war at a worse time, given the death and carnage I experienced in the early part of 1917 in the freezing temperatures of that dreadful winter. I do not wish to dwell on this grim period of my life for it pains me to do so and would, in any case, fill up far too many pages in the telling. Let me just say this. I realised within days of landing in France, that I could not face the prospect of weeks - let alone months - of that Hell. I heard other men talk in whispers about escaping, deserting the trenches, and hiding out in some quiet and rural part of France until the war had ended. For many this was idle banter, wishful thinking, bravado at best. For me, it became a reality.*

*My company was relocated first to Ypres in Belgium and, by April of that year, we received orders to move to Amiens in France. Bearing in mind my keen knowledge and love of geography, you may realise that this move excited me for two reasons. Firstly, the prospect of a company on the move gave me every hope of escaping and deserting the trenches. Secondly, our planned relocation in Amiens would place me much closer to the town of Albert.*

*I am not proud of the fact that I deserted and left my fellow countrymen behind. There has not been a day go by when I have not thought about my actions and felt a tug of compassion for the good friends that died on those battlefields. But I justify it like this. I did not start the war and I have never been a violent or aggressive man. I believe in pacifism. The war was wrong and statesmen and politicians - who cared little about the millions of lives that they were about to ruin - were responsible for starting it. Let them answer to the masses. Let them stand up now and say that the war was justified and those lives were lost in a good cause. I can live with my guilt, can they?*

*And so it was that one evening, while we were camped along the River Somme close to the town of Abbeville and I was posted on guard duty, I was able to slip away from our position and leave my company behind.*

*The weeks that followed were terrifying for me. I had to avoid capture by my own side and was reluctant to move more than a few miles each night. During the day, I kept myself hidden and grabbed what I could to eat from the trees and hedgerows once the rations I had taken with me ran out.*

*In my second week of freedom, I had the first of many lucky episodes in France. I had come across a derelict farmhouse not far from the village of Aumont, some thirty-five miles from Albert. Inside, I found a reasonable bed, some food, clothes and boots, which I guessed had been abandoned only a short time before. I also found a map hanging on the wall of the dining room, which I removed from its frame and folded up to take with me. I felt comfortable to be changing out of my uniform, donning the attire of a French peasant farmer – in reality, not much different to my farm clothes back in Suffolk. I buried my uniform, army boots and military papers and, most reluctantly, my rifle. I now had nothing on me to indicate who I was or where I had come from. In fact, my only real possession at that time was the small, black-metal key that I kept on a chain around my neck.*

*I stayed at the farmhouse for two nights, enjoying the relative comfort of my surroundings and content, for the moment, to be away from other people. But I knew that I could not stay there forever, and on the third night made plans to travel ever closer to Albert. Wrapping a number of items of food and some bed linen into a blanket, I fashioned a makeshift rucksack from some old belts and a piece of tarpaulin. It was not comfortable to carry, but it did the job and, if I were to get caught, I felt it would at least give me the appearance of a local, fleeing from the fighting. I also carried the remainder of the tarpaulin to use as a tent.*

*The days and nights that followed were not without incident, as I came across at least two French army patrols and spent most of my time hiding in ditches and taking advantage of whatever shelter I could find. Occasionally I would see other travellers on the roads and footpaths, wandering almost aimlessly, displaced no doubt by the impact of war.*

*At least the weather proved kind, remaining largely dry until I finally came within five miles of Albert. At this point, I took refuge in a small brick-built shed on a hillside beside what remained of an extensive vineyard. This appeared to be a bad choice, for the next morning I awoke to the frantic shouting of an angry, bearded man holding a shotgun. The French that I had learnt did not enable me to readily understand or communicate with this man, although I gathered from his actions that he was less than pleased that I had slept in his property. In my frustration, I shouted back at him in English, "Please, I do not understand!"*

*His reaction was remarkable and all at once the shotgun was lowered and he gave me a broad grin. "Anglaise?" he mused.*

*I nodded, reluctant to smile back in case this was part of some elaborate trap. But he seemed genuinely pacified and beckoning for me to follow him, turned and paced out of the shed and off up the hillside. I hurriedly gathered my few belongings together and staggered out after him, squinting in the early morning light and taking in the variety of aromas that filled the air that bright spring morning.*

*There can be little doubt that lady luck continued to be on my side during that brief period in France. The vineyard owner that found me was the ageing Xavier Renouf, a bear of a man who loved life and appeared to have a particular fondness for the English. I learned later that his wife, the very elegant Vanessa Renouf, was the granddaughter of an English sea captain who had settled in the region some years before. Vanessa could speak very good English and both seemed happy to take me in and feed me, proudly serving me a meal on their prized Lowestoft porcelain – a welcome reminder of home.*

*The elderly couple provided me with a bed that evening and seemed unconcerned about any risks they faced in sheltering me. The next day I rose early and after a welcome bath and shave came down to find a large breakfast waiting for me. Still the couple seemed unconcerned about this young, ill-clothed Englishman who was wandering around the French countryside in the middle of a war. But on the basis that they did not appear to be in the least bit worried, I relaxed and enjoyed another good meal with them.*

*After breakfast, I once again thanked Madame Renouf for her hospitality and said that I would be leaving within the hour. She nodded sagely and smiled. "Peter, you are not the first British deserter to pass this way. And I doubt you will be the last. I wish you well in your travels."*

*I felt some embarrassment at this, but smiled back and went off to gather my rucksack. When I said goodbye to the couple, I promised sincerely to repay them one day, and set off down the long track that led from the front of their imposing farmhouse. It was only later that I learnt how much I owed them, when I found that Xavier had hidden within my rucksack a loaf of French bread, some goat's cheese and a good bottle of red wine.*

*If you are still with me, Heinrich, you will understand that I was now within a stone's throw of the townhouse and the hoped for diamonds. Emboldened by my experience with the Renoufs, I began to walk the four or five miles towards Albert in broad daylight. The route appeared to be quiet for the most part - Xavier had indicated that the Germans had pulled back from the town at least a month before, having occupied it for some time prior to that. I hoped to God that this did prove to be the case.*

*Luckily, I encountered no soldiers of any kind and by late morning I stood on the outskirts of the town. I do not know what I expected to see at that point, but the sight I was faced with came as a big surprise. The area had been heavily shelled, with numerous buildings levelled and debris scattered all over. So bad was the damage left by the fighting, that I could scarcely work out the layout of the town compared to what I had learned back in Suffolk.*

*This was without doubt the lowest point of my journey so far, as I imagined that the townhouse in which your family had lived all those years before had been raised to the ground by the artillery shells. If this was the case, all of my efforts would have been in vain and my quest would be over. I stopped to rest at a large white gatepost that stood proudly and alone amidst the rubble of a former home, a large residence, judging by the size of the plot. Occasionally I would see local people coming and going through what remained of the town, none of them paying much attention to me. I am sure that they had more pressing concerns.*

*Having eaten some of the bread and cheese given to me by Xavier, I made my way into what remained of the town, still unsure what to do. I felt confident that I had reached the part of the town in which the house had stood, although I could not be sure. But as I scoured the buildings and rubble in desperation, my gaze centred on the remaining two stories of an impressive townhouse standing close to a small orchard. The walls of the house were dark blue and in an earthenware pot to the right of the main doorway I could see a single topiary tree. This had to be it.*

*My pleasure at finding the house was short-lived. The front door was locked and as I walked around the property on the side nearest to the apple orchard, I could see that very little of the building was still standing behind the front wall of the house. Without much thought for the dangers I faced, I began to climb over the mountain of debris. I felt strangely uneasy walking on what remained of the interior fittings and beautifully crafted furniture – one moment stepping over a child's wooden horse, the next climbing up and over what looked like a large marble fireplace.*

*I am able to recollect that scene with incredible clarity as I write these words to you. And I am sure that you will understand how elated I was when, towards the rear of the house, I looked down amid the debris and saw beneath my feet the metal casing of a small green box. Dusting off the front of the box with my sleeve, I could see a maker's name etched clearly in one corner and realised with joy that I had indeed found a safe. With the collapse of the interior walls of the house, the safe that had lain hidden for so many years, had finally been exposed – and only I knew of its existence.*

*I checked to make sure that no one was watching me, aware suddenly of the vulnerability of my situation. I tried to move the safe, thinking that it may be better to try and open it elsewhere. But even though the casing itself was less than one foot square, I could not move it at all and it remained fixed firmly among the brick rubble. I had to take a chance and open it there and then having come this far.*

*With some trepidation, I removed the key chain from around my neck and held the small safe key in my hand. I was a little surprised to find that it fitted the lock tightly and precisely and turned with relative ease - so well engineered was the lock, that I heard only a faint clicking sound as the mechanism released the bolts around the door. Gripping the small recessed handle above the keyhole, I lifted the door open very slowly until it would open no more and rested in its upright position. At first, I could see nothing inside, but as my eyes raced eagerly around the inside of the safe I saw a small, velvet-covered case, about five inches wide, tucked away in the bottom left-hand corner. I removed the case with both hands, gently rubbing its red velvet covering with my thumbs and realising as I turned it around that it was exquisitely made. The hinges and clasp of the case were made of gold and the expensive velvet on the lid was embossed with the initials 'F G D'. Jean Descartes had clearly planned your father's inheritance with every last detail in mind.*

*I confess that I could not resist the temptation to open the clasp of the case to see what lay inside. But I was not prepared for the remarkable sight that greeted me. The case contained dozens of diamond stones, of various sizes, shining and glistening like stars in the night sky. I lifted the case closer to get a better look at the gems and marvelled at the way the light on the cut stones created a rainbow of colours against the deep, blood-red silk lining of the case. I had never seen anything so mesmerising or so precious and understood in that moment how passionate and dedicated Jean Descartes must have been in his work.*

*Having finally found the diamonds, I realised that my adventures were far from over and now had the difficult task of thinking about how I might escape from France and get back to England. I even wondered if it was such a good idea to return to my homeland, given that I was now a deserter and faced the very real risk of being shot by my own side. I did not know what to do for the best and decided that I would try to find a safe haven until I could make firmer plans. But fate was to intervene once more.*

*For the first few days after leaving Albert, I began again to travel at night, sleeping where I could during the day and surviving on whatever food and water I could lay my hands on. I decided to head away from any land held by the Germans, but progress was slow and my initial caution meant that I could only travel a few miles each night. Despite my best efforts to avoid detection I was eventually caught one evening as I stumbled across a camp set up by a detachment of four British soldiers close to the village of Martinpuich. The man that discovered me hiding in a ditch was Private David Harker, a young soldier from Essex who was to save my life and provide me with a way of escaping France.*

*It happened like this. Harker continued to point his rifle and shouted at me to climb out of the ditch. He was nervous and I could see the rifle shaking. His three colleagues immediately joined him. They pulled me bodily from the trench, kicking and punching me until I passed out. When I came around I* could see that the four had searched my rucksack – the contents were scattered in the mud and they were passing round the opened bottle of red wine. As I had passed out face down, lying on my chest, they had not searched me in person and I could still feel the case of diamonds pressing into my ribs, hidden within an inside pocket of my thick smock.

I felt drowsy and weak. My chest ached and I could taste blood in my mouth. One eye was swollen and I had some trouble focusing on the four as I came around. In view of the beating I had just received, I decided to come clean and admit that I was British and a deserter, thinking (accurately as it turned out) that this might at least prevent them from searching me. They were surprisingly sympathetic to the news, at one point passing me the wine and offering me a cigarette. The oldest of the four, a sergeant referred to only as 'Simmo', explained that they would have to turn me in. "Orders is orders," he said, "...can't have you running around the countryside scaring the Germans now, can we?"

Harker explained that they were the only survivors from their original Essex company. As a result of their earlier service, they had been moved into logistics, driving a couple of two-ton Guy trucks, supplying troops at the front with much needed ammunition and supplies. Their only concern now was to sit out the war, avoid being killed and to return home to their loved ones. Simmo said that they were heading for the town of Arras the next morning, and would hand me in to a senior officer at that point. I had no choice but to go along with their plans.

That evening, Simmo built a small fire and over some food and hot tea we chatted about our various experiences of the war. I told them my background, but was careful to avoid telling them much about my movements in France and was more content to listen to their stories. Feltham and Price were single men and gardeners by trade; both had worked on a large private estate on the coast near Harwich. Simmo was also from Harwich, but married with four children. He seemed to have done a variety of jobs in a colourful and highly amusing career. Harker was the closest to me in age and had grown up in Maldon, cut off from most of the world and devastated by the exodus of working men to the battle trenches of western France. His parents had both died when he was in his teens and his only close relative was a distant great-uncle, who was serving in the Royal Navy.

The next morning, the soldiers roused me at dawn with a cup of black tea. Thirty minutes later, we climbed into the trucks heading for Arras. I rode in the second of the vehicles, between Simmo and Harker. For the most part, the journey was uneventful and we made reasonable progress in spite of the poor state of the village roads we encountered. By this stage I had grown to like both men and the three of us laughed together as Simmo told us stories about his days back home, working as a baker.

I cannot readily recollect where we were when the first explosion turned the truck ahead of us onto its side. Simmo hit the brakes hard and Harker and I shot forward. I was dazed, cracking my head on something inside the cab. I remember Simmo shouting loudly at both of us to get out of the truck and the sound of rapid machine gun fire outside. Harker jumped down from the vehicle, and then reached back in, grabbing me by my left arm and pulling me down, roughly, from the cab. I fell headlong and heavily onto the ground below at the same time as a second explosion lifted our truck off the ground and deposited it away from us to the right. I looked up briefly, to see Harker drop to his knees and then fall to one side holding his stomach. At that moment I passed out.

*For the second time in less than twenty-four hours, I came round to find myself in strange circumstances. The air was choked with thick black smoke from our burning truck, but I could hear no sounds other than the crackles from the fire near to me. Little remained of the first truck, which was, by this time, a burnt-out blackened shell. Beside me lay the body of Harker. His face was turned towards me and his eyes were staring, blankly, without emotion. I rolled him onto his back, realising that he was dead, shot through the chest by the machine gun fire. About fifteen feet in front of me, I could see the body of what looked like Price, similarly twisted and motionless.*

*I was fearful that our attackers were still close by and did my best to crawl, firstly behind the burning truck, and then into a thicket of bushes on the edge of some woods. I waited there, cold and weak, hiding for about an hour, until I was certain that no one else was around. I was not sure why the Germans had left without checking that we were all dead. Perhaps they had and wrongly assumed that I had also passed away.*

*Walking over to the first truck, I was shocked to see Feltham's charred remains, his body still sat at the wheel of the overturned truck. Nearby, Price was also dead but not burned. I guessed that he had managed to escape from the vehicle, but had been shot in the head. Despite my searches, I could not find Simmo.*

*I held no grudges against the four British soldiers, recognising that not so many weeks before, I would have been forced to do what they had done and arrest any suspected deserter. In the aftermath of the attack, I decided to bury Harker and Price in a shallow grave, having first removed their few remaining belongings, intent on returning these to their families if I could. But as I thought* more about this, I realised, from what Harker had said the previous evening that nobody but a distant relative was going to miss his death. I did not wish to dishonour the man, but realised that his unfortunate death had provided me with a good opportunity to escape my present predicament. I changed into Price's uniform and boots, which fitted me well, and put all of the men's papers and possessions into my pockets. I then buried the pair in the woods, marking the grave with a crude cross that I assembled from two pieces of wood and some wire I salvaged from the remnants of the truck. From that point on, I assumed the identity of David Harker, a soldier from Maldon in Essex.

This transformation proved to be easier and more fruitful than I could have imagined. As Harker's company had been largely wiped out during the Battle of the Somme, I imagined there would be few, if any, that would remember him. Even if they did, I could always claim to be a different David Harker – it was not such an unusual name. Given that Harker's great-uncle was serving in the Navy, I also imagined that communications with him were likely to be infrequent if they existed at all.

I walked throughout that night on towards the town of Arras, as the Essex men had originally planned. On arrival at the town and the British defences, I presented myself to a senior officer and explained what had happened, identifying myself as Private David Harker and handing him Price's papers and possessions. I also told him that to my knowledge I was the only surviving member of my company. From that point on, I was attached to a new company, fighting thereafter in both France and Italy. And all the while, I fought as David Harker and carried with me your father's diamonds.

*I hope that you will indulge me a while longer Heinrich, as I still have some further elements of the story to share.*

*My final months of the war were spent in Holland, running food supplies to troops and civilians. During this time, I met a Dutch girl called Katerina Plokker, who I very quickly fell in love with. With the end of the war, we made plans to marry and I decided that I would continue to live in Holland, fearful that any return to England might risk the exposure of my secret past. In December 1918, Katerina and I married in Giethoorn and moved into a small house given to us by her father. The marriage was well attended by Katerina's family. I stuck to my story, that the only close relative I had was a great-uncle, who was still serving in the British Navy.*

*Katerina and I continued to live happily together in Giethoorn, among the waterways and reed beds of our rural home and on 15th January, 1920 we were blessed with a son, Gerald. During this time, I began to visit the diamond dealers in Jodenbreestraat and the canal houses along the Amstel River in Amsterdam. I was cautious at first, taking only a few of the gems with me on each visit and selling these to produce a steady income. This also gave me the perfect alibi at home – as far as Katerina and her family were concerned, I was a genuine diamond dealer, carrying on the profession I had started before the war, having sold the two remaining trawlers of the Harker family fishing business.*

*In the two years that followed our marriage, I learnt more and more about the diamonds that I kept locked away at home. Most were of an exceptional quality – testimony indeed to the knowledge and expertise of Jean Descartes. But gradually, as I realised their true worth, I began to sell more and more of the diamonds, in Amsterdam and beyond, and always with the same degree of caution. I never sold more than a couple at one time and always visited new dealers during each trip. In this way, I was able to sell all of the diamonds without drawing any unwanted attention to myself. I kept detailed accounts of each transaction and deposited the money that I made from these in various bank accounts.*

*Katerina believed that I was making a modest, but comfortable, income from my business dealings. In part this was true, as we lived off only a tiny fraction of the income that I made. And from my share of the diamond money, I began to reinvest the capital in other precious stones and a number of diamond mines, turning each investment into a tidy profit. In less than two years, I was an extremely wealthy man, but was determined to ensure that I never spent more than half of the original proceeds from the diamonds, as I had promised Franz.*

*By December 1920, with all of the diamonds sold and all of my accounts up to date, I realised that the total proceeds from the sale of the gems had reached a staggering amount of money – the equivalent of £80,000. It was only when I worked out the amount in British currency, that I could appreciate what a legacy Jean Descartes had left his son. And from my reinvestment of half that amount, I had amassed even more money.*

*At this point, I took another important decision. Supported by Katerina, I decided to move back to England, to raise Gerald as an Englishman. I had enjoyed my time in Holland, but did not feel it could ever be my real home. I missed my family back in Suffolk, although I realised that it would never be possible for me to make contact with them again. They would know of my desertion and probably believed that I was now dead. I was prepared to risk exposure at this point, knowing full well that the diamonds had been sold and confident that whatever happened to me, I had made more than adequate provision for my family and could also now arrange for you and your mother to inherit the equivalent of £40,000.*

*Throughout the early part of 1921, I made the necessary arrangements for us to move from Holland to England and in March we moved into our new home - Trimingham Manor - in Surrey. All of our assets have been transferred into British bank accounts without any problems. To this day, Katerina knows nothing about my real past or the story I have shared with you.*

*In recent months, I have been trying to learn of your whereabouts in Germany, assisted by my legal advisor, Barrington Henshaw. This has not been easy as I am sure you will appreciate, given the continuing problems caused by the aftermath of war and the ongoing political upheaval in your country. However, with Henshaw's help, I was able to discover that you still lived in Hamburg, albeit at a new address. I was also saddened to learn that your mother, Nicole, died a couple of years back from influenza – I hope that you will accept my most sincere condolences.*

*In summary, you now know the full story. I have written this letter to you to set the record straight and to invite you to come forward and accept what is rightfully yours, the Descartes Inheritance. Clearly, I did not want to send you any money with this letter, for the risks that this might pose. However, if you could write back to me or make arrangements to travel to England, I will be more than happy to arrange for the transfer of the money into any bank account you suggest.*

*I intend to honour my promises to your father and will ensure that you receive all that is due to you.*

*I remain yours truly,*

*David Harker*

***********************

It was about eight-thirty that evening when Holmes finished the recital, to great excitement. For the first few minutes, Wattisfield, Curtis and I talked eagerly, astonished that such an incredible story appeared to lay behind the curious events which had befallen the manor house earlier that day. Only Holmes remained silent, his brow furrowed, as he stared up at a painting of David Harker – or Peter Coleman as we then knew him – which hung above the fireplace of the spacious room. When at last he spoke, it was with some disappointment. "This is indeed a convoluted state of affairs, my friends, and some elements of this mystery remain unclear to me."

It was Wattisfield who replied. "Such as, Mr Holmes?"

"Well, the letter was written in 1921. It seems curious that our man should wait the better part of five years to travel across to England to claim this *Descartes Inheritance*. And in doing so, he finds Harker to be deceased, which can only have added to his difficulties in seeking to obtain what was rightfully his. And knowing that Barrington Henshaw had assisted Harker in locating him, it seems odd, again, that Descartes did not appeal to the man's better nature and present the Harker letter as proof of his claim."

"I take your point, Mr Holmes, but we should be in a position to run all of that past the young valet very soon. I have arranged for him to be brought here for questioning first thing tomorrow, and Mrs Dawson has extended us an invitation to dine at Trimingham this evening and to stay overnight."

"That is most welcome," said Holmes. "Bravo, for Mrs Dawson! She puts me in mind of another very able housekeeper, for whom I had every admiration." He cast me a glance, before adding with touching candour: "Alongside your good self, Watson, Mrs Hudson was as close a companion as I ever had. Her passing was a great blow to me."

It was the first, and only, time I had ever known him to speak so affectionately of our long-dead landlady and housekeeper. In that moment, I realised that the ten years of his physical isolation and self-imposed mental introspection in Sussex had left Holmes as lonely and vulnerable as I. With the loss of my dear wife, some seven years before, I had never come to terms with living alone. And it was clear to me that for all of his upbeat banter and declarations about the virtues of self-sufficiency neither had my dear friend.

The next morning, I awoke to see the sun already warming and illuminating the large double room that I had slept in at Trimingham. When I ventured downstairs some thirty minutes later, I was embarrassed to find that Holmes and Wattisfield had been up for a good two hours and a telephone call to the manor had confirmed that Descartes was on his way and likely to be with us within fifteen minutes. They told me that Curtis had been relieved from his overnight watch over the crime scene, which made me feel doubly guilty that I had slept in for so long.

I helped myself to two rashers of bacon, some toast and a spoonful of scrambled egg from the serving dishes which Mrs Dawson had left in the dining room, as Holmes and Wattisfield sat engrossed in the headlines of the day's newspapers.

It was twenty minutes later, when I heard the bell ring loudly at the door of the manor and followed Holmes through to greet the prisoner. Descartes cut a rather poor figure, dwarfed as he was by two burly uniformed constables on either side of him. He was around five feet, nine inches tall, with black hair, a small dark moustache and matching goatee beard. His keen eyes were an intense blue hue and his gaze most piercing. On being introduced to us by Wattisfield, he nodded his head and said in a distinctly Germanic tone, "Good morning, gentlemen."

Directed by the Chief Inspector, we assembled once more in the drawing room. Wattisfield, Holmes and I sat on a large sofa to one side of the fireplace. Descartes was seated on a sofa facing us, his two guards having been directed to stand by the door. Under the watchful gaze of the young German, Wattisfield removed the Harker letter from inside his jacket and placed it very visibly on a small coffee table in front of us. Descartes sat up smartly, a look of trepidation on his face.

Holmes sought to reassure him. "Herr Descartes. Please do not be alarmed. Having read the letter, we understand fully why you came to Trimingham and the very colourful story behind your family inheritance. What is still unclear to me, however, is why you waited so long to respond to Harker's invitation and why you did not take Henshaw into your confidence on first arriving at the manor? Perhaps you could start with the letter?"

A look of anguish settled on Descartes' face. "I can tell you everything you need to know about that damned letter – a document that has forever ruined my life, despite the enormous potential it could and should have held for me. While David Harker sent the letter in August 1921, I knew nothing of its existence until six months ago. Since that time I have sought to claim only what is rightfully mine, although I now realise that in doing so, I have unwittingly placed my head inside a hangman's noose. My tale is best told from the start, gentlemen, so you would be wise to ensure that you are sitting comfortably, for there is much to tell."

Holmes smiled appreciatively and extended his left hand to prompt Descartes to recount his tale. What followed was every bit as compelling as the Harker letter.

"My name is Heinz Descartes, although my birth certificate records me more formally as 'Heinrich'. Until reading the Harker letter earlier this year, I knew little about my father, Franz Descartes, who died during the war when I was sixteen years old. At that time, I lived with my mother, Nicole, in the Altona district of Hamburg. But when she passed away in the summer of 1919, I moved into a nearby house with Aunt Hilde, one of my mother's older sisters.

"I grew very much attached to Hilde Rosen, a woman in failing health who doted on me as if I were her own. Over time, the idiopathic hydrocephalus she endured began slowly to eat away at her body and mind. Confused and subject to occasional blackouts, she became convinced, in all but her most lucid moments, that I really was her son – a role that I was happy to play along with given my own emotional deprivations.

"On the day that Harker's letter arrived, it is likely that Hilde opened it, not realising that it was addressed to me. In the two years that I had lived with her, I had never previously received any correspondence. But as she began to read, I believe she would have realised to her surprise that it was intended for me.

"Being able to read English sufficiently well to understand the opening few paragraphs and the serious nature of the communication, she would have continued to read the remainder of the letter in her private quarters – this she always did with important correspondence, sat at her bureau amid the splendour and finery of her French-style parlour. I can imagine that by the end of the document she understood enough of its contents to decide that I must never see the letter – perhaps she would not allow me to be taken in by what she believed to be a confidence trickster, who had invented a pack of lies to entice a young man to leave his home for foreign soil. But in that moment of illness or calculation, she put at risk the inheritance that was my birthright and that David Harker had struggled so hard to preserve. Whatever her motivations, I believe that Hilde placed the letter in the locked and hidden draw of her bureau, where it remained undiscovered for nearly five years.

"In the summer of 1923, two years after Harker's original letter, a second envelope arrived at the house addressed to me. On this occasion, I had intercepted the post and opened it. It was not a long letter. In fact, it was somewhat curt and to the point. It merely informed me, that as two years had passed and I had been unable or unwilling to contact Harker, the latter felt he had done all that he could to honour his promise to Franz Descartes, my father. It went on to say that if he did not receive any subsequent communication from me in the next six months, he would consider the matter closed by mutual consent. The letter was written by the solicitor, Barrington Henshaw.

"You have to understand that this letter meant nothing to me at the time. I had then only a basic grasp of English and needed some help with the translation. But I was troubled by the reference to my father. When I showed the document to Hilde, over breakfast that morning, she feigned disinterest and advised me to ignore the letter, suggesting that it was likely to be a crude attempt to extort money from us. Trusting in my Aunt's judgement, I discarded the letter, although I never forgot about it.

"Over the next year, with Hilde's health and private income both in decline, I took on a number of jobs to put food on the table. At dawn, I rose early to deliver fish from the docks to a number of the fishmongers in the Fischmarkt. Throughout the day, I worked as a wages clerk in a small brush-making factory. And at least three nights a week, I worked for a shipping firm. My wages from all three jobs were sufficient to allow us to survive in those difficult times.

"In December 1924, Hilde finally passed away, leaving her home and belongings to me. At her funeral, all but the few family members present believed me to be her son. I was devastated by the loss and unable to continue living alone in the house. I sold the property and most of the furniture, keeping only a few of Hilde's most treasured possessions including, crucially, her walnut bureau or *bonheur-du-jour* with its scarlet lacquer and gilt inlays.

"A few months later, after a number of unsuccessful applications, I was offered and accepted a position as a domestique in a large French chateau in Bourbon, in the Allier area of the Auvergne Region, not far from the City of Bourges. I was keen to escape the hardships of my home country and start a new life and career in the birthplace of my father. The bureau went with me to France and did not look out of place in my spacious attic bedroom within the *Chateau Roche*.

"Each day I worked hard at my job, learning more and more from the head of service and improving my command of many languages to better serve the family's numerous foreign visitors. Each evening, I sat at the bureau writing out my thoughts and observations in a diary. The initial hostility of the other staff to me being German was lessened by the fact that I had French ancestry, as evidenced by my surname. I was also well regarded by my employer, such that when the elderly major-domo passed away in the spring of this year, I was offered the top job, running the domestic affairs of the Roche household as efficiently as I could.

"One cold April night, as I was putting a few lines into my diary, I observed that the veneer covering one part of the bureau's inner panels, close to the three main drawers, appeared to be loose, as if peeling away from the wood beneath. I pulled gently at it with my forefinger and was surprised to find that the panel came away from its recess revealing a hidden drawer. I was excited by the discovery and amazed that I had never known of its existence. Unfortunately, the drawer was locked and I had no key, but such was my enthusiasm to discover what treasures might lie inside, that I forced the lock with a letter opener. As the small drawer slid open, I found that it contained only a single document – the Harker letter.

"You cannot begin to understand my mixed emotions reading that letter, as I did, some five years after I was meant to. My initial reaction was one of disbelief, followed closely by one of anger – anger that Hilde could have chosen to hide the letter from me, a letter that explained so much about my family's past and that connected me directly to my late father. My mother and I had received the official notification that my father had died in that fateful raid over England in 1916, along with a small package of his belongings recovered from the crash site. Reading Harker's letter, I understood clearly the pain and loss that Franz must have felt as he lay dying in that English wood.

"I could not reconcile how and why Peter Coleman should go to such extraordinary lengths to honour his promise to a dying enemy airman. And remembering the second letter that I had received from Henshaw, I felt an enormous sense of loss and frustration. If only I had made contact with Harker at the time and tried to find out more about the nature of his correspondence! A hundred questions raced through my mind as I stared out from my attic window into the darkness – Could I still put in a claim for what was mine? How could I get to England?

"The chance discovery of the letter perplexed me for weeks, although my intentions became clearer by the day. I could not allow this to be an end to the matter and leave Harker in possession of all my family's wealth. I did not challenge Harker's claim to half of the money and knew that the man had acted with the utmost integrity, but felt I owed it to my father to pursue the matter. On 25th April, my birthday, I left *Chateau Roche* for good, armed with an excellent reference and all the money I possessed. Less than one week later, I stood on English soil, planning my journey to Trimingham Manor.

"Being a cautious man, I was keen to find out what I could about the family before introducing myself to the mysterious David Harker. It was not difficult to find Trimingham Manor, set as it was among hundreds of acres of rolling countryside. But I acted with some care, booking myself into a village inn close to the manor, posing as a hill walker. In the days that followed, I chatted to many local people, learning what I could.

"I was immediately disappointed, saddened and then frustrated to discover that Harker and his wife had died overseas in a mining accident. As a result, I was told that Harker's six-year-old son, Gerald, had inherited the estate. Asked about the source of their wealth, local people knew only that the late David Harker had been a successful diamond merchant and a generous man who contributed much to support local charities. Beyond this, I could discover little else, although it was common knowledge that young

Gerald was now being looked after at the manor by an appointed legal guardian. The executor also had instructions to recruit a permanent valet for the young man, who could tend to his needs when Gerald was at home from boarding school.

"Recognising that I needed to act, I decided to visit Trimingham Manor during my second week in England. Instinctively, I approached the tradesman's entrance, enquiring at the door about vacancies for domestic staff. The housekeeper, Mrs Dawson, was very friendly and showed me into the kitchen, where I was asked to wait. When she returned a few minutes later, I was told that Barrington Henshaw, Gerald's guardian, would be pleased to see me there and then. I was a little taken aback, recognising Henshaw's name and wondering if he recollected my name from the letter he had sent me in 1923.

"I was led into what I now know to be Harker's study, where Henshaw greeted me. I was disarmed instantly by the man's relaxed demeanour, his friendly smile and the casual way he offered me a seat and a glass of whisky. I accepted the whisky and sat with him at a small marble table in the corner of the room. He explained that my timing was good, for the house was in need of a valet for Gerald Harker. Henshaw had taken on the role of guardian with some reluctance and wished only to fill the vacancy as quickly as possible, to enable him to get back to his primary role as solicitor in a local legal practice. He then asked me about my background and experience.

"Having given Henshaw an outline of my short career in France, I then produced my written reference from the Roche family, albeit written in French. Henshaw rose from his chair and paused briefly to glance at the letter, clearly unable to understand a word of it. He then extended his hand to me as I remained seated at the table and without any further hesitation, offered me the job, suggesting that I start immediately. No mention was made of my German upbringing.

"I had mixed emotions about taking on the job. It seemed that my name meant nothing to Henshaw. I imagined that if I were to confront the man with the facts about my claim, he might refute my story and have me removed from the house, effectively ending any chance I had to claim my inheritance. On the other hand, I was at least within the house, and close to all of the wealth that my family's diamonds had helped to create. Until I could think of something better, I decided to accept the new role.

"Since being at Trimingham, I have been content to serve Gerald, acting as a mentor to the young Englishman. It is a relationship I have worked hard to foster, hoping that one day I might be able to confide in Gerald and explain all that had happened in the past. Unfortunately, subsequent events at the manor seem to have deprived me of any such opportunity.

"Yesterday, I had planned to take a long walk around the estate while Gerald was out for the day visiting the boarding school that had been selected for him. Barrington Henshaw was over for the day and I told him of my plans over breakfast. Having left him in the dining room, I returned to my room to collect a small rucksack and then headed out down the drive of the estate. However, within minutes I turned and walked back to the manor, realising that I had left my new ordnance survey map on the dining room table.

"When I re-entered the dining room, Henshaw was nowhere to be seen, but as I picked up the map, I could see across the hallway that the door to David Harker's former study was ajar. Apart from the day of my interview, I had never known the door to be opened. It had been made clear to me that

Henshaw kept possession of the only key to the study and that we were all prohibited from entering the room.

"Curious to know what the man was up to, I crept across to the door and peered in. There appeared to be little light in the room, as the curtains to the study were permanently drawn, but I could see Henshaw behind a large writing bureau, illuminated only by a small green desk lamp. Unaware that I was watching him, the solicitor then stood and turned to face a small painting on the wall behind the bureau. Deftly, he removed the painting and placed it on the desk. Set into the wall, I could now see a small safe, which Henshaw then proceeded to open using a key he had taken from the top drawer of the bureau. I then watched incredulously as he began to remove bundles of white banknotes from the safe, bending to place them into his briefcase which sat open to one side of the bureau.

"There was little doubt in my mind as to his intentions and I knew instantly that this was the fortune that David Harker had sought to preserve. I was also in no mood to let Henshaw make off with the money. Entering the room quickly, I was halfway across the study before he turned to face me. I stopped instantly. The initial look of surprise on his face quickly turned to one of conceit, and he smiled condescendingly as he summed up the position he now found himself in: 'Caught like a rat in a trap, you might say, Herr Descartes.'

"He stepped out from behind the bureau and came across the room towards me. I could feel the adrenaline pumping through my body, but tried to keep my emotions hidden. 'Perhaps you could explain what you think you are doing, helping yourself to David Harker's money?' said I.

"My challenge produced an unexpected response. 'I am surprised you did not refer to the money as the *Descartes*

*Inheritance* given your desire to reclaim what I imagine you believe to be yours.' He smiled again, looking less confident than he had.

"I was determined to extract some sort of confession from him. 'So, Harker let you into his little secret did he? And having seen your client pass away with no one coming forward to claim the inheritance, you thought you could have the money all to yourself, did you?' I could see that my directness had hit a nerve.

"He was quick to bite back. 'Yes, Harker consulted with me in 1921 and asked about the legalities surrounding the potential transfer of £40,000 to a young German he had never met. Having helped him to track you down, I was amazed that you did not come forward to claim the money. I then did all I could to persuade him against further correspondence with you on the matter, but he insisted on me writing a second letter. And still you did not make contact! I was, of course, sworn to secrecy, but when the Harkers died earlier this year, I realised that I had easy access to all of the money, as long as you did not appear.' He raised his chin in defiance.

"I continued to press him. 'You knew who I was, when I first arrived at Trimingham, didn't you?'

"He scoffed at me. 'Of course I knew. A young German arrives in the village asking questions about the family and then has the audacity to arrive at the manor enquiring about a job. Didn't you think it strange that I took you on with such feeble credentials? I thought it better to have you here, working for me, until I could work out how best to get access to the money.'

"I could not resist taunting him. 'Well, it seems I have thwarted your plans somewhat, Mr Henshaw. What do you plan to do now?'

"Once more, his response was not what I expected. 'Well, I am more than happy to capitulate and let you have your £40,000, of course.' I saw that the relaxed smile had returned to his face.

"I think it must have been his patronising manner that finally brought my anger. I grabbed at the lapels on his tweed jacket and began to push him back across the room. He continued to smile at me in his sickly manner, as I gave his hapless body one final push away from me. I then watched as he stumbled and fell backwards against the mantelpiece. I was incensed that he had tried to buy me off with what amounted to my own birthright and think that he could then take what was rightfully young Gerald's. I had fallen prey to my emotions and realised all too late that my final push had killed the man. His body lay in the grate, the back of his head smashed in and a growing expanse of blood filling the hearth.

"I panicked in that moment, realising what I had done. My only hope was to try and escape and make it back to the continent. In those final moments, I counted out exactly £40,000 and left everything else as it was. I found Henshaw's key and locked the study behind me, hoping that it would be some time before anyone might find the body. I then set off and walked some miles to the nearest railway station, where I caught a train to Poole and booked into a small guesthouse. Had your men not detained me yesterday, I may well have succeeded in making the passage across to France."

Holmes opened his eyes and looked across at Descartes. He had been listening intently to every word of the valet's story, and with the conclusion of the narrative, he was quick to interject. "Chief Inspector Wattisfield and his officers have a clear duty to ensure that this matter is brought to a conclusion in the most satisfactory manner, in accordance with the laws of this land. For what it is worth, I am convinced that you have told us all of the pertinent facts in this case, both clearly and honestly. I do not believe you are guilty of murder and would say that a strong case could be made for this to be viewed, more appropriately, as an accidental death. What say you, Watson?"

I nodded in agreement, adding that justice had to be served, but could see little point in pressing for a charge against Descartes in the circumstances. Henshaw's manner and intentions had not been honourable and I imagined that none of the staff would shed much of a tear for his passing.

Wattisfield, of course, would not allow us to brow beat him into any sort of decision there and then. He busied himself with practicalities for the rest of the morning. Descartes was told that he would be kept under house arrest for the foreseeable future, in the charge of one of his original captors. Mr and Mrs Dawson were told what had happened at the same time as Gerald Harker, although the full story of the *Descartes Inheritance* was kept from them. After some telephone calls back to Scotland Yard, Wattisfield announced that a car would be arranged to take us back to Holmes' farm. By the early afternoon, the two of us were once again seated around my colleague's comfortable kitchen table enjoying a plateful of Holmes' garden produce. An hour later, I bid Holmes farewell and made the journey back to London.

*************************

It was a good two months before I heard anything further about the Trimingham escapade. I was re-reading a favourite American Western novel in my small street-facing parlour, one chilly afternoon, when I heard a distinct rat-a-tat on the front door. I knew instantly that it was Holmes, his knock as familiar to me then as it had always been in our Baker Street days. I could not hide my pleasure on answering the door.

"Watson, your passion for Zane Grey is a new affectation on your part, but I am reassured to see that you have not lost your traditional love of snooker." He swept into the hallway and continued his discourse, while removing his hat and heavy black overcoat. "I would venture that your trip to the theatre yesterday evening was marred by an argument with a taxi driver on the way home and in recent days you have received news that your application to become a member of the governing board of the Charing Cross Hospital has met with success. How am I doing so far?" he chimed.

I could but smile and, as ever, be humbled by Holmes' proficiency in observing those tiny clues which pass unnoticed by so many of us, and which provided him with the vital intelligence to see so far into the personal affairs of other men. On this occasion, I had no appetite to query how he had managed to discern so much of my recent life in such a short space of time.

"I take it that you have news of the Descartes case?" said I.

"You are not wrong, dear friend. I have just come from Scotland Yard where I was engaged to decipher an intercepted communication from a Bolshevik sympathiser in Sydenham to his Soviet paymasters. In doing so, I appear to have foiled a plot to murder the Foreign Secretary. While there, I caught up with Chief Inspector Wattisfield, who had been told that I was in the building and sought me out. He had some good news."

Holmes went on to say that the charges against Heinrich Descartes had been dropped, the lawyers acting for the Crown being persuaded that there was little evidence on which to secure a conviction for manslaughter. Descartes was free to leave the country, but had chosen to remain at Trimingham Manor and continue in his role as valet to Gerald Harker. The Dawsons were apparently delighted with the outcome.

"Very neat, Holmes," I ventured, "but how does that leave the matter of the *Descartes Inheritance*?"

"That, I cannot tell you. Wattisfield has spoken to Descartes and returned the Harker letter to him. He also gave me a copy of it, which I thought you might like to keep for your records. He made it clear that any claim Descartes may wish to make upon the estate would be a civil matter, outside the interest or concern of the police. He left it with the German to decide how the matter might be pursued."

"Then there is still some hope that this long-winded saga might yet be resolved and we will live to see Descartes inherit his birthright," said I.

"There is every chance of a legal resolution, I would say, Watson. As to whether it will come in my lifetime, remains to be seen."

His anomalous reply took me by surprise. But in that moment, I realised, for the first time in our long association, that despite his enduring professional reputation and undisputed genius, Holmes' life was every bit as fragile and fleeting as my own.

As it turned out, Holmes' prediction proved to be correct. Some years later, in the late summer of 1938 – two weeks beyond my eighty-sixth birthday - I chanced to read a small piece in *The Times* about the extraordinarily long-time a German-born valet had waited to inherit a legacy of £40,000. It appeared that when Gerald Harker had reached the age of eighteen, he had been persuaded that his valet – whom he had always treated more in the manner of an older brother than that of a servant – should receive the money, which had been held in trust by the Harker family since 1921. It gave no further details, but indicated that the two men had gone into partnership in a business venture to re-open a number of South African diamond mines.

It was gratifying to learn, finally, that the case had been resolved in such an agreeable fashion. And while it had been many years since I had had any call to document one of our innumerable adventures, I felt at that time that I owed it to Holmes to set down in writing *The Trimingham Escapade*. Unlike me, he had not lived long enough to learn of its conclusion, having passed away quietly a decade before on his lonely farm in Sussex. I dedicate this final tale to him that he may finally rest in peace.

# About the Author

**Mark Mower** is a crime writer and historian whose passion for tales about Sherlock Holmes and Dr Watson began at the age of twelve, when he watched an early black and white film featuring the unrivalled screen pairing of Basil Rathbone and Nigel Bruce. Hastily seeking out the original stories of Sir Arthur Conan Doyle and continually searching for further film and television adaptations, his has been a lifelong obsession.

Now a member of the Crime Writers' Association, Mark has written numerous books about true crime stories and fictional murder mysteries. His tale, *The Strange Missive of Germaine Wilkes*, appeared as a chapter in 'The MX Book of New Sherlock Holmes Stories' (MX Publishing, 2015) and his non-fiction works have included 'Bloody British History: Norwich' (The History Press, 2014) and 'Suffolk Murders' (The History Press, 2011).

Alongside his writing, Mark lectures on crime history and runs a murder mystery business. He lives close to Beccles, in the English county of Suffolk, with his wife and daughter.

# Also from MX Publishing

MX Publishing is the world's largest specialist Sherlock Holmes publisher, with over a hundred titles and fifty authors creating the latest in Sherlock Holmes fiction and non-fiction.

From traditional short stories and novels to travel guides and quiz books, MX Publishing cater for all Holmes fans.

The collection includes leading titles such as *Benedict Cumberbatch In Transition* and *The Norwood Author* which won the 2011 Howlett Award (Sherlock Holmes Book of the Year).

MX Publishing also has one of the largest communities of Holmes fans on Facebook with regular contributions from dozens of authors.

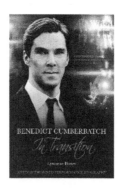

www.mxpublishing.com

# Also from MX Publishing

"Phil Growick's, 'The Secret Journal of Dr Watson', is an adventure which takes place in the latter part of Holmes and Watson's lives. They are entrusted by HM Government (although not officially) and the King no less to undertake a rescue mission to save the Romanovs, Russia's Royal family from a grisly end at the hand of the Bolsheviks. There is a wealth of detail in the story but not so much as would detract us from the enjoyment of the story. Espionage, counter-espionage, the ace of spies himself, double-agents, double-crossers...all these flit across the pages in a realistic and exciting way. All the characters are extremely well-drawn and Mr Growick, most importantly, does not falter with a very good ear for Holmesian dialogue indeed. Highly recommended. A five-star effort."

**The Baker Street Society**

www.mxpublishing.com

Lightning Source UK Ltd.
Milton Keynes UK
UKOW06f0112010216

267404UK00001B/8/P

9 781780 928449